S0-BLD-441

THE MARSF ⟨⟩ S0-BLD-441 LASSITER BROKE THROUGH THE DOORS AND FOUND THE STEER'S HEAD A FREE-FOR-ALL. MORGAN WATT WAS RIGHT IN THE MIDDLE OF IT . . .

Lassiter saw Ben Morris, his shirt torn to ribbons and his face and neck a mass of blood. A big rustler was trying to wrestle him to the floor. Watt clubbed a Bar 9 hand with a table leg and came toward Morris.

Lassiter started for Watt, but another rustler came at him from his left side, swinging a chair. In one quick motion, Lassiter turned and slammed his fist into the rustler's face, knocking him backward into the bar, where he bounced off and slid to the floor.

The marshal began to shoot into the air, demanding the brawl end. But in the noise and confusion, some concluded there was a gunfight starting. One of the rustlers pulled and fired point-blank at the marshal, putting a bullet through the side of his head.

The deputy drew and killed the rustler immediately. Other shots erupted as both the rustlers and the Bar 9 hands pulled their guns and opened fire. The marshal lay dead as stone on the saloon floor while the young deputy stared with his mouth open.

"You'd better start shooting rustlers," Lassiter advised. "There's no time to wonder about what just happened. . . ."

Books by Loren Zane Grey

Lassiter
Ambush for Lassiter
Lassiter Gold
Lassiter Tough
The Lassiter Luck
A Grave for Lassiter
Lassiter's Ride
Lassiter on the Texas Trail

Published by POCKET BOOKS

Most Pocket Books are available at special quantity discounts for bulk purchases for sales promotions, premiums or fund raising. Special books or book excerpts can also be created to fit specific needs.

For details write the office of the Vice President of Special Markets, Pocket Books, 1230 Avenue of the Americas, New York, New York 10020.

LOREN ZANE GREY

LASSITER ON THE TEXAS TRAIL

POCKET BOOKS

New York   London   Toronto   Sydney   Tokyo

This book is a work of fiction. Names, characters, places and
incidents are either the product of the author's imagination or
are used fictitiously. Any resemblance to actual events or locales
or persons, living or dead, is entirely coincidental.

An *Original* Publication of POCKET BOOKS

POCKET BOOKS, a division of Simon & Schuster Inc.
1230 Avenue of the Americas, New York, NY 10020

Copyright © 1988 by Loren Grey
Cover art copyright © 1988 Lon Garon

All rights reserved, including the right to reproduce
this book or portions thereof in any form whatsoever.
For information address Pocket Books, 1230 Avenue
of the Americas, New York, NY 10020

ISBN: 0-671-63894-7

First Pocket Books printing November 1988

10 9 8 7 6 5 4 3 2 1

POCKET and colophon are trademarks of
Simon & Schuster Inc.

Printed in the U.S.A.

LASSITER ON THE TEXAS TRAIL

LAST TIME ON THE
TEXAS TRAIL

1

THE BRAZOS RIVER RAN murky with spring runoff. It was near sundown and the western sky was dark with the clouds of yet another storm. In the mind of the stranger who watched the boiling mass rise into the darkening heavens, it was seemingly more than symbolic of the unsettled times in south Texas.

Lassiter, as ever donned in black leather, made his way to higher ground, where he hoped to find a suitable place to camp for the night. He had been roaming the vast plains for over a month, seeking work as he might find it, rousting riffraff from the dancehalls and casinos within bustling cowtowns, and riding shotgun for the new stages and freight wagons linking the settlements of this growing region.

Though the war had been over nearly eight years, the legacy of the conflict remained as harsh as ever. Lassiter found himself standing between the Blue and the Gray even yet. Land and territory was at a premium, and blood feuds settled ownership rights. For many it was a time of gain and accumulation, while others sought the trails northward, trailing herds to the railheads at Abilene and Dodge City.

Lassiter had seen all he wished of the turbulence in the growing but lawless land. It was always the same for him—never able to maintain a moment's peace—and his reputation with his twin Colts kept him always watching his backtrail.

His looks most always told those who saw him that he was no ordinary man, this stranger dressed in black, sporting two black-handled pistols. He was Lassiter and there were a lot of men who wanted to say they had taken him face-to-face. Most would never try it, though many wouldn't care if the shot entered his back—just so they could say Lassiter had fallen to their gun.

Maybe a trip to the north would bring better fortune, Lassiter thought to himself as he rode the river in twilight and watched the clouds spit shafts of jagged light into the plains. The storm was coming in quickly, wind and rain in a swirl of motion that stung the face. He huddled near a bank with his horse until it passed.

Darkness was final and Lassiter gathered what dry mesquite he could find. There wasn't much, but it offered a little light and a little comfort as the moon moved in and out of cloud banks. Coyotes called through the restless night and the constant ring of crickets echoed through blades of wet grass.

In the distance, more thunder rolled. Splashes of quick, jagged light brought the distance into focus, a distance as vast as the mind itself.

A quick plate of beans was enough to make Lassiter drowsy and he settled into his bedroll atop a small sand dune—damp, but not wet like the grass.

The storm hung across the plains, circling at will to erupt into wind and rainfall. Lassiter slept with his slicker over him, the storm a rumbling in his mind.

Finally, the threatening sky made its way into his mind.

His dream took him to the edge of a cliff, where the sky beyond spread into a sea of cattle. Longhorns moving in a line that stretched for three miles covered the plain beyond the edge of the cliff, distant and impossible for him to reach. He turned once in his bedroll. But the longhorns remained.

Why were they there? And why was he just looking across a vast expanse of open sky at them? The questions lingered and the answers wouldn't come. But as his horse finally left the edge of the cliff and joined the herd in the sky, Lassiter could see men taking shape around him.

Some laughed and some cried—some were angry and some sad. But all of them formed a ring around him and stayed their distance, as men usually did in his presence.

Lassiter turned in his sleep again as the ring of men dissolved and the herd turned. They were coming toward him, wild-eyed and bawling hideously. He awoke, hearing the ground under him rumbling. He shook himself awake as the rumbling grew louder. He jumped from his bedroll and in the darkness, he knew what was coming toward him.

With quickness fueled by the will to live, Lassiter saddled his horse and threw on his belongings. He was in the saddle and riding through the darkness as the herd wound down toward the river in a huge, bawling mass of hooves and clattering horns.

Mixed among the sounds of the herd was the yelling and shooting of range hands and Mexican *vaqueros*, screaming in their efforts to turn the herd and settle the longhorns down. The storm had set off the stampede and there was an all-out effort to stop them.

Every foot of running meant lost pounds and lost money at the trail head.

Lassiter found himself riding full-out through the darkness, the night air whipping his face. He kicked his black stallion into a dead run to avoid the onrushing herd. The yelling and the bawling and the clatter of horns just behind him, Lassiter rode with his mind working on what he must do.

Seconds seemed to drag into hours, but he stayed in the lead, ahead of the mad rush, and all sounds were lost in the trampling thunder of the longhorns. The moon peeked out now and then to allow some vision, but darkness and the shadows of mesquite thickets haunted Lassiter's perception of what was just ahead.

Finally, Lassiter was able to see that there were cowhands coming up on the herd from both sides, as flashes in the darkness told him they were using their revolvers to signal where they were to each other. Lassiter realized he had to get to the edge of the herd and be out of the way when the cowhands began their attempt to turn the lead steers into one another and thus slow down the stampede. But the herd was so crazed yet that there was nothing that would stop their surge forward.

As he held his black stallion with the pace of the herd, Lassiter drew his pistol and shot in front of the steer running right next to him. The flash and the noise scared the steer into slowing down, but it did not turn him. So wide was the front of onrushing cattle that Lassiter knew the end steers would have to be turned inward to slow them at all.

Lassiter then held his breath as he saw himself and the herd fast approaching a mesquite thicket. There was nothing to do but duck and hold onto the saddle horn as Lassiter's horse and the herd next to him crashed into the thicket with a smashing and crunching of limbs and thorny branches.

Horns rattled and the sounds of bawling cattle filled the thicket, but the herd barely slowed. Lassiter emerged out the far side, thankful his black leathers were thick enough to keep the thorns from driving themselves too deep into him.

After crashing the thicket, some of the herd started to scatter. But they were brought together with the main stream of bawling longhorns again by cowhands riding up to the left point. Lassiter, now on the right point, was joined by some cowhands who were whirling their rain slickers and thrashing the steers in the face in an effort to turn them.

Lassiter used his own slicker and thrashed the faces of the lead steers. He succeeded in slowing them and finally they turned into the main stream of the herd, the outward group on the right point carrying the others into a circle which began to turn inward on itself.

For a good period of time, Lassiter and the cowhands continued to contain the herd, letting them mill and twist and turn in a churning circle until, finally, they began to settle down. It was just approaching dawn.

In the crack of light over the eastern horizon, Lassiter saw little sparks that were cigarettes coming and going from mens' lips. The herd wheezed, as did the horses. With the rising sun came a final settling of the herd, and the men began to gather around Lassiter and whisper among themselves regarding the stranger who wore two guns and sat his horse so confidently. It was not often they saw a man obviously used to gunplay who was also so skillful at handling runaway cattle.

"I'm obliged to you, stranger," said a man who rode forward from the line of hands. They gave him clearance, as he was obviously the trail boss. "You saved my herd. The least I can do is fill you with coffee and a hot meal, if you have a mind."

Lassiter heard the voice and his mind brought forth recognition. He searched for a short time longer until he could put a name to the voice. He smiled to himself in the darkness.

"You seem quiet," the trail boss said. "What have you got to say about my offer?"

The trail boss rode a ways farther toward Lassiter, close enough to show his friendly intention, yet far enough to respect his privacy. He studied Lassiter and cocked his head when he saw the twin Colts.

Lassiter smiled once again. There was enough moonlight now for Lassiter to be sure of the man.

"Sure, I'll take you up on it," Lassiter finally said. "Just so you aren't the cook. I've never known a man yet who could keep one of Ben Morris's meals down for very long."

It took an instant before the trail boss broke into a beefy laugh. "Lassiter, is that you? It can't be. But who else would know about my cooking? And the way you sit your horse . . . I should have known."

Lassiter laughed with him and extended his hand as Ben Morris rode to him and leaned forward in the saddle. "It's been a long time, Ben," Lassiter said. "And Utah's a long ways from here."

"What's in hell's name are you doing in this country, and out here all alone?" Morris asked.

"Just traveling north," Lassiter answered. "You know me—I can't stay in one part of the country too long."

"Yeah, I know you," Morris said with a nod. He turned to his men and extended his arm toward Lassiter. "You'll find no one who can use a gun like this gentleman. He can shoot both eyes out of a rattler in less time than you can blink."

"That's laying it on pretty heavy, don't you think, Ben?" Lassiter said.

"The truth's the truth," Morris said. "Unless you've changed. And I doubt that."

"I know nothing else," Lassiter acknowledged.

Most of the hands left to round up the strays that had veered off from the main herd during the stampede. Lassiter helped trail the largest group of longhorns back to the original bed grounds, nearly five miles upriver. The storms were now gone from the plains as a smooth morning wind curled through the damp grass, bringing the rising sun.

The herd moved easily, plodding through the morning. Some of the *vaqueros* began to sing in Spanish. Lassiter told Morris about his time in south Texas, doing odd jobs that met the need of a man with a gun, a man who would bow to no other.

It was the kind of job Lassiter had come to know well and perform with precision. But when the news was out that he had settled somewhere for any length of time, there would come the strangers looking to test him. That was when Lassiter knew it was time to move on.

Lassiter then learned from Ben Morris that he was trailing cattle for the huge Bar 9 Cattle Company. The Bar 9 had a contract to deliver two thousand head of prime beef to the railhead at Dodge City, where they would be shipped to points east for butchering and processing. The sound of honky-tonk music was already ringing in Morris's ears, but he hadn't found the early part of his drive easy going.

"Don't know what to expect in this country at all," Morris remarked as they settled the longhorns in and started into camp from the herd. "Neither the weather nor the people are all that predictable."

"Doubt that will ever change out here," Lassiter said matter-of-factly. "People come and go and never really settle. And there's those who like to prowl like wolves and wait for easy pickings."

They got into camp and Lassiter could see Morris and his cowhands better in the light of the fire. Besides the stocky build Lassiter could easily see, Morris had the same penetrating blue eyes that Lassiter had remembered from years past, and the quick movements, making a man wonder if he wasn't always in a hurry. He had the same little nod to his head when he spoke something he felt was profound. And he still had the eye for detail, which came out when he asked to see if Lassiter had started notching his pistols.

"That's not my style," Lassiter said. "You count numbers too high, and you're bound to fall sooner or later."

"I've never known you to count or to fall," Morris told Lassiter. "And at this point in time, you're just the man I was hoping to run into."

2

THE COWHANDS STAYED a distance back and watched Lassiter closely for a time. They didn't crowd Lassiter as he talked to their trail boss. They knew it wasn't polite to listen in on a conversation between old friends, unless invited, and they didn't know what to make of the twin Colt revolvers and the black leather.

Lassiter noted that the trail hands were young. Most of them weren't yet twenty, with a few of the more seasoned hands close to thirty. You could tell it by their faces, for most of them had been on their own for nearly five years.

They wore wide-brimmed hats and homespun cotton shirts, with neckerchiefs above their collars. Over their cotton pants they wore chaps, or leggins, made of heavy leather, and boots that boasted high riding heels and spurs with rowels made for strong horses.

Their saddles were also made mostly at home and showed the high cantle and strong pommel needed to hold the rider in the saddle against thrashing longhorn steers. Their dress showed that they had been on the trail for some time and were already tired of storms and stampedes.

There were three Mexican *vaqueros* and the rest were Anglos. Lassiter didn't bother to study them all, for most of them were eating in a hurry; they would be catching fresh horses from the *remuda* soon to resume the drive up the trail. Sleep would have to wait until sundown came once again.

Lassiter drank coffee while Morris moved around camp, urging his drovers to take heart, saying they would get an extra long night of sleep if they could make up the ground they had lost and get that much closer to the Trinity. The stampede—and other trouble on the lower end of the trail—had cost them precious time.

Lassiter could see that Ben Morris was the same person he remembered from their previous time together. Just after the war, Lassiter and Morris had worked together on a ranch in Utah, a new ranch that was located in a fertile valley. That valley had drawn others who wanted the land.

There had been a lot of blood spilled there, as much as anywhere else a man might want to make a start. Range wars, big and little, had erupted throughout. When the sides were drawn up, there were those who preferred to stay in the middle. But when it seemed to suit their best interests, they would take sides.

Morris had saved Lassiter's life from a backshooting bartender in a small saloon. It had been close, very close, and Lassiter had always been grateful.

Lassiter noted that the hands also respected Morris and offered no backtalk. But at the same time they didn't seem to think they should be afraid of him. Lassiter figured the cowhands were young and as of yet didn't realize age could give a man an edge.

But Lassiter could see the reason for their convictions about Morris. To Lassiter's trained eye, the man's movements seemed to have mellowed some with the years. You couldn't be mellow and get a herd up the Texas Trail to Dodge City.

Other than that, Lassiter couldn't see where he had changed much at all. His features were a bit more drawn, but just a little bit, and maybe there was just a tinge of gray here and there in his dark hair. But other than that, he was the same old Ben Morris and Lassiter began to feel at home with his old friend right away.

Morris was obviously at home with Lassiter as well. But the other hands were much more reserved. The cook, a short and lean man they called Whiskey, didn't know whether to smile or frown at Lassiter. He was up in years and his sharp blue eyes were offset by graying eyebrows and hair. He chewed on pieces of root all the time as "medicine" for whatever ailed him. He said he had learned a lot from the Cheyenne.

Now Whiskey was eyeing Lassiter and chewing on a piece of root. His slim jaws worked hard and he squinted as he rubbed the stubble of his beard. He had mixed up just enough biscuits to throw in with the beans for the hands and at seeing Lassiter, knew more biscuits would be needed.

"Whiskey," Morris said to him, "this is a good friend of mine, Lassiter. He's the one who helped save the herd."

"Better eat fast, stranger," Whiskey said to Lassiter, "Or you'll be washin' your own dishes."

Whiskey hobbled back to his wagon, favoring a leg Morris said had taken a Cheyenne arrow when he was a young man fighting with the Cheyennes. Now he was old and hardened. Nobody, twin Colts or not, put any fear into Whiskey any more. He would as soon die as grovel for anybody.

Lassiter waited until the drovers had been served,

then took a plate from Whiskey. The old cook avoided any eye contact and hobbled over to the river to fill pails with water. Lassiter worked on his plate, sopping the bean juice with a biscuit. He listened closely as Morris related the circumstances of how he got to be trail boss of a cattle drive to Dodge City.

"I was like you, drifting, when I heard about John Sain's Bar 9 Cattle Company," Morris related. "I needed a grub stake and went to work. He liked me and put me on top of the bunch. Now I'm trailing beeves for him at a good wage."

"You struck pay dirt," Lassiter said. "Don't botch it."

"I couldn't find a better outfit to put in with," Morris continued. "Old John Sain, he treats me right. There's a lot of hands who are doing worse. Most wish they had my job."

Lassiter glanced up from his meal. "I would imagine. Anyone wanting to get close to a big cow outfit would look to put you down a few notches."

"I've got to be watching all the time," Morris said. "I started this drive less than two weeks ago and things have gone downhill on me already. I've lost stock to storms like this one, and to border thieves. Ran into a patch of real hell just out of San Antone."

It'll get worse farther up the trail," Lassiter said. "I hate to cause you worry."

"Don't think I ain't already worried," Morris said. "I've lost men as well as stock already. Two were killed in the roundup down on the Rio Grande by raiders after the herd, and three have quit since then. I'm shorthanded, Lassiter. I guess that's what I'm saying."

Lassiter knew very well what Ben Morris was saying. And Lassiter realized he owed Ben Morris. If it hadn't been for Morris's quick hand up in Utah, there would have been no tomorrow.

"So you need a hand or two, do you?" Lassiter asked his old friend.

"If I could get you, I'd have about what I need," Morris replied. "A cowhand and gunman to boot. It's worth double wages to me."

"Will that put you out come payoff time to the others?" Lassiter asked.

"It will save me money, if you was to come along," Morris said matter-of-factly. "We wouldn't lose the beeves we would otherwise, that's for sure."

Lassiter finished his plate and nodded. "I was headed north anyway. It might as well be for some pay."

Morris whooped, causing heads to turn. "Hot damn!" he said. "We're on our way now."

Though Morris seemed more than pleased, Lassiter wanted to clear up one very important point with him before he totally committed himself to the drive. And that was the matter of horses. The *remuda* was the bread and butter of the drive and there had to be enough horses to go around.

Each of the cowhands should have from four to six head to ride, more ideally, providing they were all well cared for and not footsore. Now Lassiter worried that if he used Ben Morris's horses and rotated them with his own black stallion, there might not be enough for both of them.

Lassiter had noticed the night before that the *remuda* was not too well stocked. It didn't appear that there were enough horses to provide for even three per man at the present time.

"We lost some horses when we fought that bunch of thieves outside San Antone," Morris told Lassiter.

"But we've got enough and we'll pick up some more when we reach Dallas."

"You're sure I won't cause you more trouble than I'm worth?" Lassiter asked with a grin.

"There's bound to be trouble for me on this drive," Morris said. "But with you along, there would have to be a lot more to throw the odds off."

"You've got another hand, then," Lassiter said, extending his hand to Morris. Then he raised his coffee. "Here's to a smooth ride to Dodge City."

Morris raised his tin cup and clacked it against Lassiter's. "Here's to hoping we even *get* to Dodge City." After breakfast the herd was brought to its feet and the drive was on once again. The sun burned through the sky and the stampede of the night before began to take its toll as longhorns and horses alike dragged their feet and slowed to rest often.

Lassiter rode point with Ben Morris and caught up on Morris's life after Utah. Lassiter had never expected Morris to stay with the cattle business, as he had been far better educated than the average cowhand. But it seemed Morris had been restless as well and had finally found something to his liking in driving cattle herds for John Sain's Bar 9.

"Since coming out here, I've always wanted to ranch a herd of cattle," Morris confessed. "I know you think just because I was raised by wealthy parents in the East, I should have turned to something more refined. But you knew me in Utah and you'll see I'm the same—I just can't keep from moving around. And there's nothing like driving these beeves up the trail. It's just that there's so much else that's not pleasant that goes along with it."

Lassiter could understand that Morris could do as well as most against hard men and hard times—no matter his upbringing—but that he needed to stimulate his mind as much as he could. Naturally, Morris was far more articulate than most and prided himself in the reading of a good book on occasion. When winter hit the northern slopes and the snow made getting around difficult, Morris would settle in with a book while the others fought over poker games and keno.

This, Morris told Lassiter, allowed him to keep his sanity. When the same things occurred day after day with the same men, there had to be some form of diversity to keep his mind fresh and open to new ideas.

"And what would *Gulliver's Travels* have to do with herding beeves to Dodge City?" Lassiter wondered aloud.

Morris grinned, "I'm never sure what to expect along this trail. Just about anything can happen."

Lassiter and Morris then talked some about the trail ahead. There were a lot of stories that were being told around campfires about the number of cattle now going up and the number of thieves looking to make off with some easy money. Morris had heard a lot about this and it troubled him greatly.

"Most of these cowpunchers I hired have never been up the trail," Morris complained. "If we ride into a mess of thieves again like we did down below, I'll likely lose the whole bunch of them."

"Where do you expect to find most of them?" Lassiter asked.

"I hear they're bad near Doan's Crossing," Morris replied. "And up along the Canadian. But you can't ever tell where they'll hit you, or how."

"They have a lot of different ways of working," Lassiter agreed. "Maybe I need to scout ahead a little and see what kind of activity has taken place ahead of us."

"That would suit me just fine," Morris said. "Whiskey will be taking the wagon ahead before long. Maybe you can go ahead of him a ways and find us a campsite."

Lassiter nodded. He rode up to where the old cook was yelling at his team of mules as they worked themselves through a small washout, holding the reins tightly so they wouldn't jump and tip the wagon.

When the wagon was safely across, Lassiter rode up to one side. The old cook ignored him.

"I'll be going ahead with you," Lassiter told him. "Maybe we can find a good campsite for tonight."

"Lucky me," Whiskey said. He bit down hard on a root. "Do you figure to shoot the snakes off the trail for me?"

"Just spit on them, Whiskey," Lassiter said. "When word gets out, there won't be a rattler left in Texas."

Whiskey grumbled something under his breath and chewed hard on the piece of root. Lassiter rode along beside the wagon in silence. After a few minutes, Whiskey turned to him.

"I suppose you shoot them fancy irons of yours off like you do your mouth."

Lassiter grunted. "What have you got against me, Whiskey? I just met you this morning."

"All your type are the same," Whiskey said quickly. "You'd sooner shoot a man than just stand and talk with him."

"It sounds to me like you've got a case against somebody," Lassiter said. "But leave me out of it."

"I seen your type gun down kids no older than the ones workin' this drive," Whiskey hissed. "And they laughed. Yeah, they laughed about it like they was big men. I tell you, I don't like your kind."

Lassiter took a deep breath and stretched in the saddle. Then he turned to Whiskey and his voice was hard.

"Do you think it would be fair if I said all trail cooks shoot women in the back?"

Whiskey turned immediately. "What the hell are you talkin' about?"

"I saw it happen with a trail cook up in Abilene," Lassiter said. "This cook gave a kid a piece of gold and sent him to the whorehouse. His mother heard of it and came by and cussed him up one side and down the other. When she turned to leave, he shot her. Double load of buckshot, right in the back."

Whiskey was silent. He chewed on his root while the mules ambled on and the harness leather creaked with the wagon wheels.

"So, I guess all trail cooks do that," Lassiter added. "Am I right, Whiskey?"

"Hell, no!" Whiskey yelled. He thought a moment. "I guess I wasn't fair to you, either, at that. What did they do to the cook?"

"Hanged him."

Whiskey nodded his approval. Finally he turned to Lassiter. "I don't aim to be so harsh as all that. It's just that we got one of those types along with us."

"Who's that? Lassiter asked.

"Morgan Watt is his name," Whiskey answered. "I don't know much about him, except that he's sure trouble. He's kin to old John Sain and to my way of thinkin', he ain't nothin' like John. But I figure Morris had to hire him since he was kin to John and all."

"Did Ben hire him as a shooter, like he did me?" Lassiter asked.

Whiskey nodded. "And he likes to kill. I don't know all about it, you'd have to talk to Morris. I just know he's trouble and there ain't no room for more of that on this trail."

"Well, please don't include me in Morgan Watt's

category of people, if he's the type of man you just described."

"I'll figure not to," Whiskey said, rubbing his stubble of beard.

Lassiter extended his hand. "We're friends then?"

Whiskey shook Lassiter's hand. "I guess you ain't so bad after all."

"Good," Lassiter said. "You seem all right to me as well." Then he chuckled and started to ride ahead to look for a campsite. "But just warn me in advance next time you intend to serve me some of your biscuits."

3

LASSITER TOOK HIS TIME moving up the trail. He had just passed where it turned off from the Brazos and headed due north for the Trinity. There had been a great deal of cattle already moved through, and the sandy ground was pocked with hoofprints in a wide swath.

With the large amount of cattle being driven to market, Lassiter was certain there would be a number of thieves around who would be looking to make a cut from the herds. It wasn't that hard to take a brand and change it to something else, especially when the prices at the railhead for beef on the hoof made such practices lucrative.

After following the main trail for some time, Lassiter rode off to the west a distance and picked up trails left by groups of riders that wound out from the main trail, often through brush or along the banks of arroyos. Men traveling in hiding. Men who didn't want to make themselves obvious.

Lassiter was certain these trails could represent

future trouble. From the look of it, some had been made by Indians who had jumped the reservation. Many of them were vicious and after blood to avenge their relatives who had been killed by whites. But they were in small groups and for the most part would leave large herds and a lot of men alone.

But other signs indicated there had been men around other than Indians, who had spent time branding and moving smaller groups of cattle. Lassiter found a lost running iron at one campsite, and patches of singed hair were strewn through the grass and among the ashes.

Lassiter was now convinced there were any number of thief gangs operating up and down the trail. But there was no way to tell just how many of them existed and when or where they would strike.

Toward late afternoon, Lassiter found a suitable campsite. There was plenty of grass and water to last overnight, and the open area could easily hold two thousand head. After scouting the entire surrounding area for nearly two miles in diameter, Lassiter felt confident there would be no trouble here.

Whiskey arrived with the cook wagon and set up for the evening meal. He told Lassiter he had been thinking about their conversation early that morning.

"I ain't figured how you can be a shooter like you are and not like to kill," he said.

"Some shooters, like myself, get started out of circumstances they had no control over," Lassiter told him. "The war bred a lot of ugliness and there are times when a man has to do what he thinks is right, no matter what somebody else might think." Whiskey nodded in agreement. "I hear that. Things ain't never what they seem."

Whiskey went ahead with his preparations for the evening meal as the herd came over a rise not far to the south. Lassiter rode to meet Morris and tell him what he had discovered regarding thieves along the trail.

"How much do we have to worry about right away?" Morris wanted to know.

Lassiter gave his opinion. "It looks to me like a group of them already made off with some beeves, branded them, and are likely in Abilene now, or some-place close, selling them. I didn't see any fresh tracks today, though. I think we've got a clear trail at least to the Trinity."

Morris and the hands settled the herd in for the night and then gathered around Whiskey's wagon for his evening offering. Beef and beans went down easily. They hadn't eaten since early morning and all were ready for a good meal and a long night's sleep.

There was an air of tension in camp, though, and Lassiter sensed it right away. Throughout the day the cowhands had been discussing Lassiter and sharing their observations of him. And though it was obvious to all of them that Lassiter was somebody special to Ben Morris, not many held it against him. But there were a few—and one in particular.

Whiskey had been right about Morgan Watt.

Morgan Watt never looked a man straight in the eye unless he intended to kill him. Then it was for reasons of intimidation. Watt was a first cousin to old John Sain, the owner of the Bar 9. When Watt had sought Ben Morris out, Morris had had no choice but to hire him. To help protect the herd, was how Watt put it. He was supposed to make sure the beef got to Dodge City.

Watt had a reputation as a gunman in south Texas and seemed to have something on John Sain. Though Ben Morris got along well with John Sain, there was no room for questions when old John insisted that Watt be hired on for the trip to Dodge City.

Lassiter learned more of Watt from Morris as they turned their horses into the *remuda* and made their way back for supper. Morris said he had noticed the tension building throughout the day and had heard some of the cowhands remarking about comments Watt had been making.

Sundown would come soon and over late evening coffee, Morris told Lassiter that Watt was boasting that he intended to show everyone that he was the top gun on this drive. According to the gossip Watt intended to drive Lassiter away—and do it the first thing after supper.

Lassiter sipped his coffee, "Are you going to back me if Watt tries something?" he asked Morris.

"I don't like Watt," Morris answered. "You know I don't like him. Just the same, he's kin to John Sain. And you know the old line about blood and water."

"That allows Watt free rein to trample over anybody then?" Lassiter asked.

"I'm not worried about you," Morris told Lassiter. "I just want you to give him some leeway. Maybe he'll see that he shouldn't mess with you and leave well enough alone."

"Is he brash enough to draw?" Lassiter asked.

Morris nodded.

"I don't intend to let him shoot me," Lassiter warned.

"Just make sure everyone knows he started it," Morris said. "I'd hate to have to tell old John that someone shot his cousin, but I figure if I work for the Bar 9 long enough and Watt stays with the outfit, I'm going to have to bury him sooner or later."

"How many are you going to have to bury nurse-maiding Watt?" Lassiter asked him.

Morris took a deep breath and swallowed some coffee. "I don't intend to bury anybody," he finally said. "But don't push him, that's all I'm saying."

"I don't intend to let him push me around," Lassiter said. "I'll respect your wishes the best I know how, but I know his kind. They just don't quit until it's too late."

Suddenly one of the hands burst into camp on his horse. It was the wrangler, a Mexican *vaquero* named Felipe Martinez. He saw Morris and talked hurriedly from the saddle.

"*Senor* Morris, you must come quick," he said. "Two of the men are fighting over a horse. I cannot stop them."

Morris set his tin cup down and turned to Lassiter. "We'll discuss this further when I get back."

Lassiter nodded and watched Morris hurry out toward the *remuda*. He noticed Morgan Watt a short distance away, smiling to himself.

That morning, after the stampede, Lassiter had noticed Watt but had thought little of it. At the time, Lassiter had caught Watt staring at his twin Colt revolvers. Nothing new or different, to Lassiter's way of thinking. But now Watt was paying particular attention to his own pearl-handled modified Colt Army .44, which he kept sparkling clean.

To date, Watt had killed six men in disputes of various types. That was the justification John Sain gave Morris in hiring him. Though Morris knew he was a troublemaker, old John Sain had insisted he go along. Morgan Watt could use a gun, there was no question. But he made situations happen where he could justify to himself the use of his gun.

Lassiter usually paid men of Watt's caliber little mind. He saw them all the time, following him like camp dogs at a butchering. But he knew he could ignore Watt no longer. Lassiter realized that to Watt's way of thinking he represented a threat to his position in the form of a stranger with twin revolvers, dressed in black leather.

Watt watched Lassiter refill his cup of coffee. Watt wasn't as tall nor as broad as Lassiter. But Watt considered himself better with a gun. And under those circumstances, size doesn't matter.

Watt waited until Whiskey left the cook wagon to gather wood for his morning cookfire. He watched Lassiter lean back against a wheel of the chuck wagon. The time was now right.

Watt advanced with his thumbs in his gunbelt and studied Lassiter with a hard eye.

"Care for some coffee?" Lassiter offered.

Watt grunted. "This ain't no social call, stranger." His voice was low and gravelly, but loud enough to turn everyone's head.

"What kind of call is it then?" Lassiter asked.

Watt cocked his head to one side. "You seem to know horseflesh pretty well, don't you?"

Lassiter sipped on his coffee. "As well as the next man," he replied, meeting Watt's gaze.

"Well, I saw you eyeing my roan," Watt said in a louder voice, so that everyone was sure to hear. "I don't want you to think he's yours, 'cause that's the way you looked at him."

"Are you sure you've got that right?" Lassiter asked.

Watt nodded slowly, his thumbs still in his gunbelt. "I'm plumb sure of it," he drawled.

"You're wrong," Lassiter said. "I just thought that good roan needed a better rider, whoever it might be. He's good horseflesh for sure and he ought to have better on his back."

Watt's mouth fell open. He had never in his life had

anyone speak to him in that manner, ever, and it took him aback for several moments. Finally, he cleared his throat.

"You sayin' I ain't fit for that horse?"

"You tell me," Lassiter replied. "And you tell me why I'd eye your horse when I've got one twice as good."

Watt shifted his weight from one foot to the other. He hadn't planned that Lassiter would turn things so easily on him like that. He was certain Lassiter was right in saying his big black was better than the roan. And Watt knew if he called Lassiter on the remark and challenged him to a race, Lassiter's horse would win going away. Now he had to try and turn things back around.

"I just think you're tryin' to start trouble," Watt finally said. "Maybe you're just a troublemaker."

"I'm standing here minding my own business and you come over to tell me about your horse," Lassiter said. "Maybe I don't care to hear about your problems."

Watt was digging himself in deeper and he knew it. He finally decided the only way he was going to win this one was to accuse Lassiter of not merely eyeing it with envy, but actually planning to steal the horse.

"That trouble out there that Morris went to take care of ain't got nothing to do with the two hands he's talking' with," Watt said in a loud voice. He was looking at Lassiter with a crooked grin. "One of them heard somebody wanted to take my roan. He just went out to make sure that didn't happen. I think Morris ought to know you caused the trouble and just run out."

"If you know so much about it, why don't you go tell Morris how it is?" Lassiter challenged. "Or maybe you're afraid he'll laugh at you, like everyone else does."

Watt stiffened. Lassiter didn't seem to get angered by anything. And now Watt was being made a fool of and he didn't want to allow Lassiter to run over him like he was—not without settling things his way.

Watt now he resorted to the only thing he knew— gun talk.

"I just think you want everybody to see those big Colt pistols of yours," Watt said. "Just because you wear them doesn't mean you can use them."

"How'll we know for sure?" Lassiter asked Watt.

Watt licked his lips. Most men would become frightened. But this stranger, who took him so casually, showed not even the slightest hint of tension in his whole body. It bothered Watt to the extreme.

Lassiter continued to sip his coffee, but lowered his right hand to just above the butt of his revolver. It wouldn't take both hands to deal with Morgan Watt.

At the same time, Watt slipped both thumbs from his gunbelt and let his arms hang at his sides. His eyes worked on Lassiter, but Lassiter was almost smiling.

"You've gone mute," Lassiter prodded. "Either speak or act, or forever quit bothering me."

Watt went for his gun. His hand was still frozen to the butt of the pistol when Lassiter's Colt was cocked and leveled at his midsection.

"Feel like dying, Mr. Watt?" Lassiter asked him. "Believe me, the next time you aim to pull a gun on me, you'd better be able to do it.

Whiskey had returned and was now standing just off to one side. He set his two pails of water down on the ground and stared at Lassiter. He had seen the whole thing, and had wondered at Lassiter's blazing quickness.

"Why don't you shoot him?" Whiskey asked Lassiter. "He would have you."

Lassiter sipped from the tin cup again, his eyes and his pistol still on Watt.

"I'm waiting for his next move."

His fingers trembling, Watt released the butt of his revolver and turned his eyes downward.

"There's no need for anybody to die," Lassiter finally told Whiskey. "I think Mr. Watt here is well aware now that his gun isn't as big as he thinks it is. And if he really wants to help get John Sain's herd to Dodge City, he will reserve his anger for those who come after the herd."

"When John Sain hears about this, there'll be hell to pay," Watt snapped. "We're kin, and he won't take kindly to it."

Whiskey was looking hard at Watt now. He considered the fact that Watt had certainly started the trouble, but he didn't know the reason. But he knew that since Watt was kin to John Sain, there could be some friction between Sain and Ben Morris over this incident. Especially since Morris had hired Lassiter.

Whiskey realized that John Sain respected his opinions on matters, as he had cooked for the Bar 9 for over three years. And after his discussion with Lassiter that morning—and seeing now that Lassiter hadn't taken advantage of the situation and shot Morgan Watt—he would need to let Watt know there were those with influence on the drive who would side with Lassiter and Ben Morris.

"You were hired to help keep the herd from thieves," Whiskey told Watt. "That's what Morris hired this stranger for as well. So why you two fightin'?"

"He's a horse thief," Watt said of Lassiter. "He'd have my roan if he thought he could take her."

Whiskey looked to Lassiter as Lassiter took another sip of coffee and carefully slid his black-handled Colt back into its holster. Lassiter then turned to Whiskey and frowned.

"Is this man as much trouble to everybody else, or didn't he get his milk this morning?"

Watt tensed again and his hand went back to his revolver.

"Just remember what I said," Lassiter told him. "If you draw . . ."

Watt's face was dark red. His hands were shaking with anger. Lassiter watched him closely for a time and then, deciding Watt shouldn't get off without learning a lesson, told Whiskey that he didn't like being called a horse thief.

"I wouldn't either," Whiskey said. "Them's shootin' words where I come from."

"I don't think Mr. Watt wants to try shooting any more," Lassiter said. "But I wonder if he'd like to try his luck with his fists?"

Watt licked his lips again. He was not going to back down, no matter what happened. He had been made a fool of and to ignore Lassiter's challenge would be to face certain loss of respect among the cowhands, no matter how good he was with a pistol. He took off his gunbelt.

4

LASSITER TOOK OFF HIS GUNS and walked out away from the chuck wagon. He stood confidently and waited for Watt to make his move. Watt was angry enough to kill, but he realized he was in for the fight of his life against this stranger.

The hands had gathered around them and were watching intently. Watt was hoping Lassiter would tire of waiting and would come at him. But Lassiter was content to hold back calmly and show that Watt was the aggressor throughout the whole incident.

When it appeared Watt wasn't going to start anything, Lassiter commented on his hesitation.

"It seems to me that you've bitten off more than you can chew, here," Lassiter told Watt. "Do you feel like quitting while the quitting's good?"

This enraged Watt even more and he came at Lassiter, moving quickly and striking out with determination. Watt was quick, but Lassiter easily dodged two of his blows with surprising quickness. He then blocked the third one with his forearm, coming back with a right cross that knocked Watt's head back and sent him tumbling to the ground.

Dazed, Watt rolled to his side and wiped smears of red from his mouth. He shook his head and worked his way to his feet. He was breathing heavily already and his crushed lips were still oozing blood. But he saw the eyes of the cowhands on him and he decided his valor was at stake.

Watt came at Lassiter again, but with more finesse. He was determined to make some kind of mark here, and that meant killing this stranger.

Watt showed more skill and determination than before, but was still not able to land a good blow against Lassiter. His fists were either blocked or bounced off Lassiter's broad shoulders. It was as if Lassiter were giving him a chance to back off and keep from getting himself busted up worse.

But Watt wasn't about to back off. He finally became totally frustrated and picked up one of Whiskey's Dutch oven cooking pans. Lassiter backed away while Watt swung the heavy cooking skillet wildly. Watt kept missing and finally threw himself off balance with a crazy swing. Lassiter then stepped in and slammed his fists into Watt unmercifully.

The first blow slammed into Watt's ribs. He gasped and dropped the Dutch oven. Then Lassiter leveled a savage blow into his stomach, which doubled him over. Watt was cursing and telling Lassiter he was going to kill him. Lassiter then took him by the hair and pulled his head up, sending a heavy fist into Watt's face.

The blow caught Watt just below the left eye, opening a deep gash and cracking the bone. Watt groaned with the impact and spun backwards into a heap on the ground. He lay moaning, having nearly lost consciousness.

Lassiter stood back from Watt and looked around at the various expressions on the cowhands' faces. Nobody spoke a word and all expected Lassiter to finish Watt then and there.

Instead, Lassiter turned away. Whiskey picked up one of his water buckets and carried it over to where Watt lay on his stomach. After turning Watt over, he dumped the water into his face.

Watt pushed himself up to a sitting position and started cursing again, shaking the water from his hair and face. The cowhands were still staring as Lassiter calmly walked over to the wheel of the chuck wagon and fastened his two gunbelts around his hips.

"What's going on here?" came a voice from behind them.

Everyone turned as Ben Morris pushed his way through the hands to the middle of the circle. Watt was just coming to his feet.

"I should have known," Morris said to Watt. "You didn't waste any time, did you?"

Watt fought to get his breath. His anger was rising again, as if he didn't have the good sense to know when he was beat. He pointed to Lassiter, holding the side of his face.

"He came at me, Ben, for no reason. Send him out of camp, or I'll tell John."

Whiskey, as well as a number of the other hands, began to speak up immediately. Whiskey then told Morris the story and Morris asked Watt why he couldn't just leave Lassiter alone.

"I don't have to answer to you, Morris," Watt spat, his voice filled with hate, his face swelling from the beating. "But don't think old John won't hear about it."

"John put *me* in charge of this drive, Watt," Morris

retorted. "See to it you remember that, if you intend to stay on, that is."

Watt was now strapping his gun back on. When he was finished, he replaced his hat and glared first at Lassiter, and then at Morris.

"I'm stayin' on, for sure," he growled to Morris. "And don't think I don't aim to set things right."

He turned then and shouldered his way past the hands and out to the edge of camp. Morris told everyone the show was over and that they had best get some sleep and get ready to rise early. The Trinity was only a couple of days away and Dallas would be the last stop before they made the drive up to Dodge City.

When the cowhands had dispersed, Morris got another cup of coffee and took Lassiter aside. Lassiter could see that Morris was concerned about what had happened and the implications of what could occur farther up the trail.

"What did he say to you?" Morris asked.

"He accused me of wanting his roan horse," Lassiter answered. "It was all planned and crazy to boot. I think he just wanted to see if he couldn't get me riled."

"He's trying to get the whole bunch against you," Morris said. "He told those two hands I just broke apart a pack of lies."

"Lies?"

"About you," Morris replied. "It sounds like Watt wanted them to think you were after their horses as well."

Lassiter thought it more than coincidence that Watt had confronted him at the exact time Morris had gone out to see what the trouble was over horses in the *remuda*.

"I suppose he told them I was figuring some plan to get their horses, too," Lassiter guessed.

"That's just what he told them," Morris said with a

nod. "But he twisted it and made it seem like each one was trying to sell the other one's horse to you."

Lassiter looked up from his coffee. "So he had them against each other and me as well. He made them both think I was sneaking around trying to get one to sell the other one's horse to me."

"That's it," Morris said with a nod. "I'm still not sure if they don't believe that."

"That would be a crazy thing to try and do," Lassiter said with disgust. "No one could ever get away with that."

"These hands are young, Lassiter," Morris pointed out. "Someone like Watt can get them stirred up pretty easily. And their horses are something they don't want to have someone else fooling with."

"Maybe if I'd known this," Lassiter commented, "I wouldn't have been so easy on Watt."

"From the looks of him, you didn't do him any favors."

"I should have made it worse. Say, no teeth and a mouth swollen shut so he can't tell any more lies."

"He'll think more about it next time," Morris said. "I don't think he made any friends here tonight."

"Let's hope you're right," Lassiter said. "I figure by the time the sun comes up, most of these hands are going to have their minds made up about Watt, one way or the other."

"Just get a good night's sleep," Morris told Lassiter. "I want you thinking more about the troublemakers outside of camp than the ones here among us."

Lassiter nodded and started for his bedroll. In parting he turned once more to Morris.

"On the other hand, the troublemakers here in camp might prove to be worse than the ones we haven't met up with yet."

*   *   *

Dawn brought gunfire and Lassiter was quickly out of his bedroll with the others. He had his pistols ready when someone yelled that it was just Morgan Watt taking target practice.

Most of the hands grumbled, worried that the herd could stampede again if Watt wasn't careful. It was lucky they were just rising from their bed ground and the day was open and bright. Had it been evening or during a thunderstorm, there would no doubt have been another stampede.

But no one was going to say anything to Watt about his foolishness. None of the hands wanted anything to do with Watt after the night before. His left eye was swollen shut and his face was black and blue from his lips to his forehead. They were all afraid he might turn his gun on them.

Lassiter thought seriously about telling Watt to use more discretion about shooting around the herd. But that would certainly incite Watt into more anger and there would be gunplay. Lassiter didn't want to have to kill Watt, not after the altercation the night before. It would look too much like he had goaded Watt into the fight and Ben Morris would suffer in the end if John Sain took offense.

So everyone stayed clear of Watt and Watt kept his own distance. Whiskey had more beans and fried beef ready for breakfast, plus a treat. He had gathered some berries from the bushes growing in a nearby draw and had made pudding. There wasn't enough for more than just a small portion for each man, but the taste would stay with them most of the day.

Watt didn't bother to eat any beans or beef. But he did take some pudding and stood right in front of Whiskey and spit a mouthful onto the ground. Everyone watched as Whiskey's face clouded with anger. But no words were spoken.

While Whiskey got the breakfast dishes cared for, the cowhands all hurried to the *remuda* to catch their horses. Watt stood back and Lassiter watched him, sulking on the edge of camp, planning something while everyone else got ready for the day's drive.

Lassiter finally decided Watt was digging his own grave as far as the Bar 9 cowhands were concerned and finally joined the others to catch his horse. For the time being everyone forgot about Watt and went to the work of the day. There was a herd of two thousand longhorns to worry about.

Lassiter formed a lariat with his rope and stood back with the other hands while the horses came toward a rope corral. Martinez and another hand helping him emerged from a cloud of dust and pounding hooves. The leader of the horse herd entered the corral and the entire herd then began to mill about, while Martinez and the other hands got ready to catch their horses for the day's drive.

Cowhands in turn entered the corral and with their loops dangling beside them, chose their horses. It took little time, as each hand could cast his loop with accuracy, over backs and rumps and heads of other horses, to settle neatly around his own horse's neck.

The dust was immediately so thick as to render the visibility next to zero. And the horses became instantly wary. If the hand missed getting the loop over his horse's neck the first time, he always found it hard to make a second throw count. The horses would then dodge and hide among the others in the herd, turning and twisting and doubling back to avoid being caught.

But in a relatively short time the cowhands had caught and saddled their horses, Lassiter among them. And now came the time for the show, for there were some horses who weren't inclined to be ridden right away.

Lassiter's black stallion had pride and spirit, but the animal was not so green as to need the kinks ridden out of him. Other hands worked to stay in their saddles as their horses pitched and bucked. The hands laughed and whooped when an occasional one of them would be flipped from his horse and have to get up, dust himself off and try again.

Finally, the horses were all ready to work and the herd was moving up the trail. After a short discussion with Morris about the camping spot for the next night, Lassiter got ready to scout the country around them again for thieves. He noticed Watt had settled in with the other hands, pushing the herd across the vast open.

The cattle were beginning to string out in their customary long line that would eventually trail back for three to four miles. Whiskey was already getting a headstart to bring the cook wagon ahead for the evening meal. Lassiter rode up alongside once again to visit.

"I'm obliged that you put in for me last night against Watt," Lassiter said. "You didn't make Watt your friend by doing that."

"Watt's never been my friend and he never will be," Whiskey said. "Next time I make puddin', I'll poison his."

"You took it pretty well," Lassiter complimented him.

"I don't know about next time, though," Whiskey said. "I'm old and cantankerous, and I could get myself killed."

"Just play it easy," Lassiter suggested. "Don't let him get under your skin."

Whiskey reached into his pocket and pulled out a piece of root. He bit into it and chewed until a piece came off, then stuffed the rest back into his pocket.

"I'm a bit worried about Watt," Whiskey then said. "He's startin' to make me nervous."

"Do you think he means to cause more trouble?" Lassiter asked.

"A lot more trouble," Whiskey answered. "And soon."

5

LATE THAT NIGHT, THE HERD was settled in near a draw filled with fresh water. The men in camp seemed more relaxed than they had been for nearly a week. The reason was clear—Morgan Watt was not around.

It happened some time during the day and Morris had no idea where Watt had taken off to, nor did anyone else in the outfit. He hadn't mentioned that he intended to quit. He seemed to have just drifted off sometime during the day without attracting a lot of attention. Most hoped that he had decided he didn't want to stay with the herd now that Lassiter was riding along.

Lassiter had been up ahead, scouting the country just south of the Trinity. He had seen no sign of Watt anywhere along the trail, or anywhere off where he had been scouting. Nor had Whiskey, who had taken the wagon on ahead and was waiting when the herd was settled.

It wasn't until well after supper, when everyone was getting ready to find their bedrolls, that Watt showed up. He was riding at a leisurely pace as if he had done nothing unusual.

Lassiter noted that the hands were talking among themselves, expressing their disgust at Watt's actions. Had it been one of them who had wandered off to do whatever he pleased, he would likely be fired.

But they knew Watt wouldn't suffer that kind of fate. He would merely tell Ben Morris he could do what he wished and Morris would go along with it. Lassiter wondered if that would be the case, or if Ben Morris would decide he had had enough of Morgan Watt.

Watt took his time rubbing down his horse and turning it loose into the *remuda*. He strolled into camp whistling and with all eyes on him, came over to Whiskey's chuck wagon.

Lassiter watched while Whiskey offered Watt some dried biscuits and beef. Watt held the tin plate in his hand a few moments and tossed the biscuits and beef off onto the ground.

"Can't I get something hot?" he asked with a scowl.

"You're too late for supper," Whiskey said, working to hold his temper. "And you don't treat what you got with much respect, so you can't be all that hungry."

"So, you're not goin' to fix me anything? Is that it?"

Whiskey chewed hard on the piece of root in his mouth. "You ain't gettin' nothing until you pick up them biscuits and beef you threw away. And if you don't pick them up, that could be for the rest of the drive."

Watt grunted and turned around to face Morris and Lassiter. Watt ignored Lassiter, but when he tried to step around Morris, the trail boss stopped him.

"Where the hell were you today?"

"I had to go someplace."

"Well, you'd better tell me where, or you can go right back there permanently."

Lassiter was both glad and relieved to see that Morris wasn't going to put up with anything from Watt. Watt was now going to be forced to answer his questions, under threat of being fired. And if he didn't answer anything, the other hands would be witness to the fact he had left without proper authorization.

"I need to know where you were," Morris persisted.

"You can't fire me," Watt growled.

"I told you before, old John put me in charge of this outfit," Morris corrected him. "I'll fire you whenever I want. You can take it up with John. I don't care. Now, I want to know why you just up and rode off without telling me. We're shorthanded as it is."

Watt jerked his head toward Lassiter when he spoke. "You've been sending him up ahead all the time. I just thought you'd best be wary of your backtrail as well. You never know when somebody might sneak up and take what they can from the stragglers."

"You were behind the drag, watching for thieves?" Morris asked.

Watt nodded. "But I didn't see anything."

Lassiter thought to himself that Watt had likely been behind the herd, but that it wasn't surprising that he hadn't seen anything. Maybe he hadn't really been looking. Maybe he had met with the thieves.

"If you were worried about our backtrail, why didn't you tell me you intended to look things over?" Morris asked again. "I could have sent someone with you."

"I don't need someone with me," Watt snapped. He pointed to Lassiter again. "You don't send no one

46

with him. Besides, you said you're shorthanded with the herd.''

"Next time, you tell me where you're headed," Morris said flatly. "Otherwise, you can check out the trail all the way back down to San Antone if you want. And you won't be getting paid for it.''

Watt didn't say anymore to Morris, but glanced sideways at Lassiter with a look of deep hate. The marks on his face from the beating Lassiter had given him seemed to puff up that much more as he moved the jaw muscles underneath. The anger was intense, and seemed ready to boil over.

Lassiter couldn't understand why this man had— from the very first day—suddenly and without question developed such a dislike for him. Lassiter could only surmise it had to do with something that had not yet developed. Perhaps Watt was involved in something that would have happened a lot easier had Lassiter not joined the trail drive—something that Lassiter could figure to put a stop to.

After glaring for a time, Watt moved off into the semi-darkness, where he placed his bedroll at the edge of camp and retired for the night. The few hands who had remained up to tell stories around the fire now left for their own bedrolls. Tomorrow would be upon them soon enough and there was bound to be trouble now, for that seemed to be Watt's middle name.

While the next few days passed and the herd moved, Lassiter kept his eye on Watt and concluded the gunman was waiting for the right time and the right place to enact a plan he was dreaming up. There could be no other reason for his sudden relaxed nature.

There was no way to know where Watt had gone or what he had been doing during his day's absence. But Watt seemed sure of himself about something.

He paid little attention to anybody and seemed to gain more confidence all the time. His face was still puffy, but now the dark color was receding, leaving a reddish-pink tint where the blackness had been and a heavy dark scab where Lassiter's knuckles had cut him under the eye.

Lassiter knew something was going to happen that would prove Watt had been up to no good the day he had dropped back from the herd. It was only a matter of time until Watt would show his hand to everyone.

It happened near mid-morning of the day they would reach the Trinity. Once across the river, Morris had promised the hands a short stopover in Dallas. There were supplies to pick up and he wanted to send a message to John Sain that they were going up the trail and all was well.

As Lassiter and Morris discussed the plans for the stopover, a number of stray cattle drifted into the herd. It wasn't all that unusual to have cattle drift into a herd—especially this close to Dallas and Fort Worth—but they were cattle that seemed not to belong to anybody.

The cattle bore a brand Morris was not familiar with—a Double D 6 on the right hip. Morris considered himself very familiar with all the brands in Texas and was confounded at these longhorns, which seemed to just arrive out of nowhere.

Lassiter discussed it with Morris and concluded that the cattle were likely drifting from another herd as a result of the recent thunderstorms that had caused all the stampeding. There was that possibility, or the possibility they had been stampeded by thieves.

"Down below, when they got to us, they just charged into the herd," Morris was saying of the trouble just outside San Antonio. "They rode in shooting and yelling. Maybe that happened to somebody just west of us and the strays are still drifting."

"That's a common way to rustle cattle," Lassiter agreed. "But there might be some thieves around here with some more interesting tactics."

No matter whether it was storms or rustlers, it wouldn't be long, they concluded, until somebody showed up looking for the longhorns that had begun to mingle with the herd, some two hundred head or more.

Watt seemed to pay particular attention to them. He noted carefully where they had come from and how many made their way into the herd. He had been on the side where they had been drifting out of the brush and into the open.

Whiskey had gone ahead with his chuck wagon, as had the *remuda,* under Martinez's direction. They were to have camp ready on the south side of the river and after the meal, the herd would cross. Everything was set up well. The plan was to get the herd settled and allow the men to go into Dallas in shifts for an evening of fun before the longest part of the trip to Dodge City.

But soon a dozen riders came into view. Lassiter immediately knew they were associated with the strays that had joined the herd. He watched as the riders approached, noticing as the other hands from the herd gathered, that Watt was once again absent.

The riders came to a stop and a big man who had been leading them gave his name as Johnson. He mentioned right away that they had come to get their cattle back. He wore a big Colt, which seemed to be well cared for, and he eyed Lassiter for a long time.

Morris introduced himself to Johnson as the trail boss for the Bar 9. Johnson didn't seem that impressed. He mentioned again that he wanted his cattle back.

"I know we lost nearly five hundred head," Johnson said. "And they must have all worked themselves into your herd."

"There weren't five hundred head that came into this herd," Morris said quickly. "More like two hundred."

"Exactly two hundred and twelve," one of the hands interjected. "No more, no less."

Lassiter watched while Johnson looked at the hand and then back to his men. They were all sitting their horses nervously, awaiting the next move.

Johnson then turned his attention back to Morris. "I'd like to cut my stock out now."

"I know you've likely been looking for these beeves for some time," Morris said. "But I don't intend to stop the herd and lose two hours here."

"What do you mean?" Johnson asked. "You ain't leaving with our cattle."

"In just a couple of hours, we'll have the herd at the river," Morris explained. "You can inspect them then and cut those out with your brand on them."

"We ain't got the time to wait," Johnson said.

"Nor do we," Morris said. "I've got to keep this herd moving. It's a lot easier for you to trail two hundred head than it is two thousand. You can make a lot of time, and faster than we can. I think you can wait until we hit the river."

"First off," Johnson said, correcting Morris, "there's five hundred head in your herd, not two hundred. And we need to get them back—now! Maybe if we was just to cut five hundred head from your bunch, we could call it even."

"There's nothing even about any of it," Morris said, becoming angry. "When we hit the river, you can cut all the cattle out you can find with a Double D 6 on the right hip. The rest are Bar 9 stock. Got that?"

Johnson turned to the other two hands, who sat their horses without moving. Then he turned his attention to Lassiter.

"You know how to use them black-handled pistols of yours?" he asked.

"Do you really want to find out?" Lassiter replied.

Johnson studied Lassiter for a time and could find no weakness in the gunfighter's hard stare. The men behind Lassiter and Morris seemed as hard and determined to hold the stock until they reached the river. Johnson saw no use in pushing things at the time.

Johnson snorted and wanted Morris to know that he was entirely put out over the matter. He didn't think it was ethical to hold the cattle until they reached the river.

Lassiter had been wanting to ask Johnson if they could prove the Double D 6 brand was even registered. But instead he decided to ask him if he had any friends who were not present.

"I thought Morgan Watt would be with you," Lassiter told Johnson.

Johnson blinked, showing Lassiter that Watt was in with the thieves. But Johnson wasn't going to give anything away if he could help it.

"Who's Morgan Watt?" he asked.

"I thought you might know him," Lassiter finally said. "Maybe I was wrong."

"We've wasted enough time," Morris finally said to Johnson. "We're pushing the herd up to the Trinity. Be there if you want to cut out your cattle."

"Have it your way, then," he told Morris. Then he looked at Lassiter. "I guess we have no choice but to comply with your wishes. But I can assure you, we'll be back. And there'll be a lot more men with me next time."

"You're welcome to your cattle," Morris explained. "There is no argument about that. But you can't just come and tell me when you intend to cut them out. Like I said, they'll be waiting just a ways up on the Trinity."

Lassiter watched Johnson straighten up in his saddle as he prepared to turn his horse. He was watching Lassiter just before he spoke to Morris.

"We'll be up on the Trinity to get our beeves," Johnson said. "You can count on that. And they'd better all be there for us, or you can expect trouble."

52

6

WHEN THE DRIVE WAS UNDERWAY again, Morris told Lassiter that he was going to fire Watt.

"Will you back me?" Morris asked. "He might want to kill me."

"I will have to face him sooner or later," Lassiter said. "It might as well be sooner."

The drive went on without incident, though Lassiter was ready for trouble at all times. The lead cattle reached the river in mid-afternoon. Lassiter rode with Morris and three other hands to swing the herd across. The water was swift, but shallow. And for the rest of the day, the herd crossed in bunches and spread out to graze on the other side without any troublesome incidents.

After all the herd had forded, Morris had the hands go through and cut out all the Double D 6 longhorns and hold them in one area, separate from the others. There were no more than the two hundred and twelve head that had come into the herd initially, and they grazed peacefully nearly a mile distant.

Morris felt that going to the trouble of cutting out the stray cattle was more than a lot of trail bosses would do and if Johnson didn't like the numbers he saw, then he could bring on his hard men and have his trouble. Once they saw Lassiter use a gun, they would turn tail and ride back where they came from.

But Johnson never did show up—nor did any of the men who had been with him. Missing also was Morgan Watt. He hadn't shown himself at all and by now everyone was certain he was tied in with the men who had come earlier in the day demanding cattle—men who were no doubt rustlers.

The cowhands talked some of Watt and the riders, but their main concern now was getting into Dallas for some fun before it got too late. They would have to be back to the herd and ready to go again by first light; and since a lot of them would likely straggle back just before dawn, there were those who wanted to see the sights before it got too late.

"I'm going to let Whiskey go in for supplies first before I let everyone else start their crazy antics," Morris told everyone at the evening meal. "Then you'll go in bunches. You'll have to draw cards to see who watches the herd first."

The hands immediately went to their cards and began to settle the issue of who went first. While they were playing, Lassiter approached Morris. He could remember the one thing above all others that always made Ben Morris come home without even a dime to his name—gambling.

"Maybe you'd be better coming back with the herd after you pay the men," Lassiter suggested. "I don't want to sound strong to you, but I can remember Nevada pretty clearly. If I remember right, a lot of men died over a card game one afternoon."

"I can handle myself," Morris said defensively. "You just worry about the money you get."

Lassiter nodded. There was never any future in trying to tell Ben Morris anything.

By the time the evening meal was finished, Morris had decided he would allow the first group of hands to go into Dallas together. But he had made the bunches smaller and was going to allow them less time than he had originally intended. He was still worried about Johnson and the thieves showing up to stampede the herd.

Lassiter stood near the chuck wagon when Morris came over to discuss what they should be worried about, since no one had yet showed up for the Double D 6 cattle. Lassiter was as concerned as Morris and wondered if the rustlers weren't indeed planning a night raid.

On the other hand, Lassiter knew it wouldn't likely happen so close to town. It could have happened back along the trail, where they had first met Johnson and the other rustlers. But to try something where almost anybody could show up would be foolish.

"Why are you so at ease over this whole thing?" Morris asked Lassiter. "I smelled real trouble coming out there today. And since Johnson and his bunch didn't show in the daylight, I wonder what lies in store for us during the darkness hours."

"We can't take any chances," Lassiter agreed. "But there isn't a real risk in any rustlers starting things so close to town."

"What if those cowhands were real and they bring the Texas Rangers out here to tell them we stole their cattle?" Morris asked.

"If I don't miss my guess," Lassiter told Morris, "I wouldn't be surprised if there is no such thing as the Double D 6 outfit."

"But you can see the brands on those beeves plain as day," Morris pointed out. "How can you wonder if such an outfit exists?"

"I can put any brand I want on a cow," Lassiter said. "But that doesn't mean it's registered. You told me yourself you had never heard of the outfit before."

"Yes, but there's a lot of new outfits coming onto the range. I can't keep track of them all."

"Check their papers then," Lassiter suggested. "The next time someone comes along who wants to cut cattle from your herd, no matter what the brand is, be sure they can prove they work for that outfit."

"That stands to reason," Morris said. "I guess I've got some things to learn about being a trail boss."

"I would think you'd have papers of your own," Lassiter said.

"Everyone knows John Sain's Bar 9," Morris said emphatically. "There isn't anybody who'd question that mark on any beef going up the trail."

"You should still have proof of who you are," Lassiter pointed out. "If I was a trail boss and you lost cattle in a stampede that settled in my herd, you wouldn't get them back until you could prove you worked for John Sain's Bar 9 outfit."

Morris nodded. "I can see your point. So who do you figure owns the Double D 6 longhorns we've got with our herd?"

Lassiter was looking out to where a group of riders were coming toward camp. "Looks like we might find out soon," he said. "Better have the men ready to ride and shoot if the need arises."

Morris yelled for the men to get ready to mount up and defend the Bar 9 if need be. The hands all checked their guns and held their horses, waiting for Morris's signal to climb into the saddle and ride out to the herd.

But the riders, as they came ever closer, showed

themselves to be friendly. The lead rider held his hand
up in peace, Indian style and, kept it there until Morris
and Lassiter rode out to see who they were.

It was a curiosity to Lassiter to have just been
talking about Texas Rangers and then have them show
up.

Lassiter and the lead rider exchanged glances and
small grins. Lassiter was now certain that there was
going to be no more trouble with the so-called Double
D 6 Outfit.

"My name is Jack Chapman," the lead rider said,
as he took Morris's hand. "That fellow you have riding
with you, I believe his name is Lassiter. Am I right?"

Morris laughed. "You're as right as right can be.
How do you know him?"

"He can certainly attest that we're Texas Rangers,"
Chapman said. I've tried to get him to ride for us for a
long time. Maybe someday."

Lassiter nodded. "Maybe someday."

Chapman grinned. Lassiter noticed his lean dark
features had remained almost the same, taking on only
a few lines from weather and age. The man was still
tall in the saddle and commanded respect. He would
likely never quit riding with the Rangers until somebody put him in a grave.

Lassiter noticed how Chapman looked him over,
still grinning. The man had wanted him to ride with
them in the worst way and had bent over backwards
to see that he was given a good outfit. But Lassiter
was never one to stay on long, and he knew it would
be hard to leave the Rangers once he had signed on.

"You've taken to punching cattle?" Chapman then
asked Lassiter.

Lassiter nodded and motioned toward Morris. "I'm
catching up on trail stories with my old friend here."

"Stories are the fabric of the trail," Chapman said to Lassiter with a grin. "Just don't tell any on me."

"What brings you through?" Lassiter asked him.

"The matter of some stolen cattle," Chapman answered. "There's some rustlers who took a bunch of beeves from over in the panhandle and rebranded them. Most of them got away in a stampede the other night."

"That brand wouldn't happen to be a Double D 6 on the left hip, would it?" Lassiter asked Chapman.

Chapman smiled again. He looked around to the men riding with them. They were all nodding and when Chapman turned back to Lassiter and Morris, his smile was even broader.

"Seems like we've finally found what we've spent over a week in the saddle looking for. How did you come into these cattle?"

"Two hundred strays ended up in our herd today," Lassiter explained. He told Chapman the events of late morning and that afternoon, emphasizing the hands whom they had met and what they looked like— including the leader.

"Johnson is not his real name," Chapman said. "It's Clyde Wilsall. And he's been a thief since he was weaned."

"We just about had to pull our guns to stop those hands from rousting an extra three hundred head off us," Morris put in. "It could have been bad if Lassiter hadn't called their bluff."

Chapman turned to Lassiter. "I don't suppose they knew who you were, or they wouldn't have been so foolish."

"They didn't say and I didn't care one way or the other," Lassiter answered with a smile. "A cheat is a cheat, and he's bound to pay sooner or later. They just didn't feel it was their lucky day, I guess."

"That sounds a lot like what has been happening up and down the trail," Chapman said. "This bunch is well organized."

"They were supposed to show up here just after noon," Morris said. "But we haven't seen them."

Chapman turned to his men and they talked about the riders they had spotted earlier in the day, who had scattered at their approach.

"Sounds like you might have saved us a gunfight," Morris told Chapman. "You're welcome to all the beef and beans you can eat, and a soft spot in the grass to throw out your bedrolls."

Chapman smiled. "We're obliged. We might just get the first good night's sleep in over a month. Could we get a look at those beeves first?"

"I'll take you to the herd," Lassiter told Chapman. Before leaving, he turned back to Morris. "I can stay with the herd and a few men if you want to head into Dallas and pick up those supplies."

"Good idea," Morris said with a nod. "I don't want the boys out too late anyway. The sooner we get started, the quicker they will have spent their money."

Morris gathered the hands and announced what was to happen. They accepted the news with a loud chorus of cheering. With the Rangers staying with the herd, there was no chance of thieves, and that meant they could go into Dallas in bigger groups and not have to come back as soon.

Lassiter watched while Morris led the hands in a fast gallop from camp toward town. In less than an hour they would be waiting outside of some bank while Morris went in to draw twenty dollars in gold apiece for them, their wages thus far in coming up the trail.

Before it got too late, most of them would have visited the women they wanted and drank or gambled the rest away. Then they would be ready to earn the rest of their wages to blow in about the same amount of time once they got to Dodge City.

While they looked over the stolen cattle, Lassiter discussed the rustler problem along the trail and how much worse it was farther north.

"They get away with it a lot easier up there," Chapman was saying. "Once you get into the Indian Nations country and out where there's nothing to stop the thieving, they're everywhere like flies, and just as hard to shake."

"Ever hear of a gunhand named Morgan Watt?" Lassiter asked.

After a moment's thought, Chapman nodded. "He's better known south of here. He's put in with thieves all along the border. You say he's up here now?"

"He's with this outfit," Lassiter said, refilling his cup and Chapman's as well. "Morris tells me he's kin to John Sain."

"I didn't know that," Chapman said. "That's something, now isn't it?"

"It makes it hard for Morris," Lassiter said. "But Morris thinks he should have Watt along, to keep the rustling down."

Chapman was shaking his head. "The way Watt works, the rustling gets worse whenever he's around."

"That's what I was afraid of," Lassiter said. "I just wonder how much Watt knows about these stolen cattle. He wasn't anywhere around today when we had that trouble."

"I'd watch him close," Chapman said. "I don't have a warrant, or I'd relieve you of your trouble. He's a hard one to pin down. He usually goads the other man into the fight, then draws and kills him. Looks to everyone then like self-defense."

"You've got him down pat," Lassiter said. "I just know there's something about this stolen cattle thing that makes me want to keep Watt tied inside the chuck wagon. But I guess I'll have to be content to just watch him close."

Chapman finished his coffee and headed for his bedroll. He intended to take the stolen cattle into Dallas and have them penned up until their rightful owners could come and claim them. He wanted to have his men get an early start.

Whiskey was back from getting supplies. Besides Whiskey, Martinez and two others had stayed behind with the herd. None of them wanted to blow their money in Dallas. The younger hands had ambitions of their own to operate cattle ranches some day. It was a good plan, if it could ever come true for them.

Lassiter decided he would go into town for a short while and see what was happening with the men and with Morris in particular. Morris had talked all day about poker games and Lassiter knew his old friend was going to get himself plucked clean if there wasn't somebody there to watch over him.

It could be a real problem getting Ben Morris away from a gambling table of any kind. Twice in Nevada he had kept Morris from a gunfight with another card player. There just wasn't enough money in Morris's bankroll for the herd to allow him to lose as much as he sometimes did at a single sitting.

And there was somebody who had to be watched. That was Morgan Watt, who had been gone all day, and who Lassiter was certain was somewhere in Dallas, completing his plan to get the Bar 9 herd away from Ben Morris.

7

DALLAS WAS A MECCA for drifters and a hub for freight
wagons and cattle crews either coming off the trail or
getting back on the trail. Dancehalls and gambling
houses were everywhere. Cowhands wandered the
streets in the twilight, staggering and cheering, making
the rounds of their favorite saloons.

Lassiter found the Bar 9 hands in a saloon called the
Steer's Head, where half of the area was alloted for
drinking and the other half held a number of poker and
keno tables. The hands all seemed to be oblivious to
anything but having fun, in whatever fashion occurred
to them at the moment. They wanted to make it a night
to remember, for the rest of the trail would be a long,
hard pull.

They were short one more hand now without Morgan Watt. He might show up and he might not; but
Lassiter was certain that if he did, Ben Morris would
stick to his word and fire Watt.

Lassiter began to wonder what effect the absence of
Morgan Watt would have on the outfit. It was certain

there would be less tension and concern about trouble starting as a result of him, but in everyone's mind was the thought that he would surely show up again sooner or later. And then he would bring trouble.

Lassiter considered the fact that Watt was likely where he had been during his previous sustained absence—with someone who resembled the rough hands who had demanded the Double D 6 cattle be cut from the herd. It had angered all the hands at the time and there would have been gunplay had the rustler named Johnson tried to take the cattle when he had wanted them.

And among the discussion Lassiter had overheard during the evening meal, everyone seemed convinced Watt had been associated with Johnson and the others. He had just been smart enough not to show up when they were going to take longhorns from the herd.

But for now no one seemed to note, or even care about, Watt's absence. In fact, they were all celebrating and wanted to think only of having fun. Lassiter knew that most of them would do what they wanted and then go back to the herd without worrying that they had spent all their money. But there was one in particular that Lassiter felt needed some watching over.

Ben Morris had been seated at one of the poker tables for a considerable length of time. And he didn't appear to be winning.

Lassiter made his way over to the table and watched the game for a time. Morris frowned as he lost one hand after another. When he saw Lassiter, he reached in his pocket and pulled out some gold.

"Here's your wages," Morris told Lassiter. "Mind if I borrow about five dollars worth?"

Morris had been drinking a lot in a short time while he was gambling. Lassiter could tell it wasn't going to be a good night for him, no matter how you looked at it.

"Maybe you'd better pull out of the game, while you've still got something left," Lassiter suggested. "Then you won't have to borrow money."

"My luck will change," Morris said gruffly. "I'll do all right. Just give me a chance."

Lassiter could see that Morris wasn't going to be talked out of quitting the game. But Lassiter had seen games like that before and he worried that Morris might get down to nothing and after he had spent the gold he was lent, bet his horse and saddle.

"You going to lend me the five dollars?" Morris asked.

"Let me see you win a hand or two first," Lassiter told him.

"Oh, hell with you then!" Morris said, whiskey spitting from his breath. "Go do what you want. But you can count on it, I'm going to be here until I win my money back—and a big chunk to boot."

"You're the boss," Lassiter told him. "But don't get to the point where you're walking up the trail."

Morris squinted at Lassiter for a moment, then went back to his game. Lassiter ambled over to the bar and ordered whiskey, then sipped it while he watched the room.

There were any number of professional gamblers who were sitting among the cowhands and freight drivers and other patrons. There was always somebody just getting off the trail and they always had a hearty appetite for drink and other forms of pleasure.

Mixing with them all were women dressed in bright, low-cut gowns, many of them with their hair neatly tucked atop their heads. They wore various types of jewelry and adornments in their hair and around their necks, all to attract attention. They laughed and giggled and ran their hands over the men, taking drinks from them and luring them upstairs whenever they could.

Lassiter noted the Bar 9 cowhands were still scattered around the saloon, though many of them would often come and go from other nearby drinking and gambling houses. Most of them were spending their money fast in various ways and would soon be ready to return to the herd.

Morris was still gambling at the poker table, his supply of chips still dwindling. Lassiter noted a new player that had just sat in, a rough-looking hand with a deep scar on his chin. He was puffing hard on a cigar and seemed to be paying particular attention to Morris's luck.

That seemed odd to Lassiter. Morris wasn't the one winning. Most people paid close attention to the winners.

You can learn a lot about a man when you watch him play poker. Lassiter was thinking about the old adage and observing the cigar-smoking cowhand at the same time. It was obvious to Lassiter that the man was trying to figure Morris out, likely for other than just reasons of winning at cards. He still wasn't watching anyone else nearly so closely.

After a time, the cowhand cashed in his chips and got up from the table. He worked his way through the crowd and out the swinging doors. Lassiter was curious and decided to follow.

Darkness had settled over town completely, but the lights from the saloons and dancehalls lit up the boardwalks like midday. The light dimmed as it reached farther out past the boardwalks and men walked by themselves and in groups through the shadows of the streets, roving their hard-earned wages throughout the town.

Lassiter followed the cowhand to a saloon, where he entered and immediately fell in with a group of cowhands equally as hard-looking as himself. Lassiter recognized three of them as being among the men who had demanded the cattle earlier in the day—among them the cowhand named Johnson.

And right in the middle of them all was Morgan Watt.

Lassiter lost himself in the crowd and took a position where he could see Watt and the others take a bottle to a table and sit around it, pouring drinks and talking noisily. The cowhand Lassiter had followed was jerking his thumb back like he was talking about Morris at the card table across the street at the Steer's Head, and everyone laughed periodically.

Lassiter watched for a time and noted a dark-haired saloon girl who came over and took a seat upon Watt's lap. She nibbled at his ear while he talked to the other men at the table. His tones were now much lower than they had been and the cowhands were leaning over the table to hear him.

Whatever Watt was talking about had the rustlers listening intently. The saloon girl drank from Watt's glass often and then settled herself with her arm around Watt's neck.

There were a number of men at the table and when the first bottle was empty, Lassiter saw Watt talk to the saloon girl and point toward the bar. He was showing her the label on the bottle, so that she would be sure to order the same brand.

Lassiter worked himself through the crowd and hoped Watt and the others wouldn't notice him as he settled in against the bar next to the saloon girl. He could see Watt was busy talking and the rustlers busy listening to him.

It was obvious the saloon girl had been drinking for

some time and was casual with her speech and who she talked to. This suited Lassiter just fine. He knew he might get some information out of her. But he had to act fast.

"Care for some company?" Lassiter asked the girl.

She smiled and spoke to him in a low, smooth drawl. "Why, thank you, cowboy, but I'm occupied at the time. Maybe later." She giggled.

"You deserve to drink better than that," Lassiter said to her as the bartender set the whiskey bottle in front of her. He told the bartender to bring over a bottle of Old Crow, then pulled out a handful of gold coins.

The saloon girl's eyes immediately lit up. "Why, you must be rich."

"Rich is what I am," Lassiter told her. He looked into her eyes as she watched him pay the bartender for the new whiskey. "I could make you real happy."

"I hope to shout," she said. "But I shouldn't leave him, not just yet." She was pointing over to Watt.

"What's so important about him?" Lassiter asked her. "He doesn't have the gold I've got."

"So, you do have a lot of gold?" she said. "How did you get it?"

"I got rich trailing cattle to Dodge City," Lassiter told her. "I'm going to get richer. I've got another herd I'm taking up there."

The saloon girl looked over toward Watt and then back to Lassiter. "He said he was going to have a lot of money from cattle, too," she said. "He told me he would take me away with him, once he sold his cattle."

Lassiter nodded. "Does he have cattle?"

"Oh, yes. He has a big herd that he's taking up the trail to Dodge City. Just like you. He told me."

Lassiter looked over to the table where Watt and

the others were still talking. "Are those men with him his cowhands?" he asked her.

She shrugged. "I guess. He told them he didn't want to see them, though, not until Cimarron Crossing."

Lassiter nodded. "I see. He wants them to meet him at Cimarron Crossing?"

She was shrugging again. "He just said they should be there and he would meet them. I guess that's where they're picking up the cattle. That seems a little far up the trail don't you think?"

"I think it's a long ways up the trail to be picking up cattle," Lassiter told her. "Unless you intended to steal them from somebody who had already taken them that far."

She looked at Lassiter. "Do you mean you think he would take the cattle from somebody?"

"I know him," Lassiter said. "I know he would steal cattle. You had better be careful of him."

Her eyes widened. "Do you think they're rustlers?"

Lassiter turned to look over to the table and noted that Watt and all the cowhands were now staring over at them. Watt was glaring, getting ready to stand up.

"I know they're rustlers," Lassiter told her. "You wait right here while I go talk to them."

Lassiter moved away from the bar and worked his way through the crowd to where Watt was now pushing his chair back. He decided he wouldn't get up, though, and held his eyes on Lassiter.

"What's the idea, trying to take that woman away from me?" he asked.

"Is she something special?" Lassiter asked. "She must be. You told her an awful lot about what you're up to. And she told me."

Watt's face reddened and the men at the table began to get tense.

"She's drunk," Watt said. "I didn't tell her nothin'. She's just lying to you."

Lassiter turned and called the woman over. Watt and the others tensed up even more. When the girl came over, she sat the whiskey down on the table and backed away, visibly frightened.

"You telling secrets?" Watt asked her.

She shook her head. "No. He just said he was rich from cattle. And you told me you were, too. That's all. What's wrong with that?"

"That's what I want to know," Lassiter said to Watt. "What's wrong with that? So, I think you'd better be worried about getting rich with somebody else's cattle. That's not going to happen. And if any of you think it is, now's the time to speak up."

8

NOW WATT CONSIDERED THE CHALLENGE and rose from the table. He was quickly joined by Johnson, the rustler who had led the men that afternoon.

The other rustlers with them stayed put, waiting to see what would happen. The music stopped and some of the men drinking at other tables around them moved away, as it appeared there was going to be shooting.

The saloon girl tried to get away into the crowd. But at Watt's order one of the rustlers got up and forced her back over to the table.

"Leave her be," Lassiter ordered. "She's not in on this."

"She's my woman," Watt shot back.

Lassiter grunted. "Not anymore, she isn't. Let her go."

The rustler looked to Watt, who after some consideration nodded. The rustler let the saloon girl go and she backed away into the crowd.

"What do you mean by this?" Watt asked Lassiter. "You've got no business coming in here like this."

"You ran out on the herd again," Lassiter pointed out. "It seems you're spending more time away from work than at work. You're fired."

Watt bristled. "You can't fire me."

"I just did," Lassiter said. "Come back to the herd if you want, and get fired officially by Morris in front of all the hands. Maybe that's what you'd rather do."

Watt was loosening his fingers. You're pretty bold, ain't you?"

Lassiter remained calm. "Just doing my job is all."

Watt snorted. "It seems to me you do just about what you please."

"You might say that. I don't like cattle thieves."

"You ought to be careful who you're callin' a thief."

"Maybe you want to tell me you aren't one," Lassiter said. "And that those Double D 6 cattle are not stolen."

Watt lowered his hand over the butt of his revolver and tensed.

"I can't let you get away with that," Watt growled.

"Are we going to go through this again?" Lassiter said. "So far all I've heard you do is talk."

"It might be different this time," Watt said. But once again his confidence level was waning and he wasn't sure if he should start anything.

Johnson, however, didn't seem to be shaken in the least. He moved his big frame around beside Watt. He had been watching Lassiter and he had wondered ever since the incident with the cattle earlier in the day if this gunfighter was really all that fast.

Johnson had had enough whiskey to want to test Lassiter. Johnson knew he was better than average himself. He could shoot better than most—not better than Watt—but better than most everybody else. But he knew it was Watt's play now, and he was content to wait.

Watt was still considering his alternatives. If he went for his gun, Lassiter would certainly draw. But maybe he and Johnson together could take Lassiter. On the other hand, Lassiter would likely get at least one of them, and Watt wasn't ready for that.

"Maybe we should discuss this thing," Watt finally said to Lassiter. "Maybe you'd like to come in with us, given the right deal."

Lassiter cocked his head to one side and studied Watt. That was a dead giveaway. Watt was certain he couldn't win, so he wanted to see if bribery would work.

"What kind of deal?" Lassiter asked.

"We might figure something out," Watt said.

Lassiter knew Watt wasn't sincere about getting him in with them, but just wanted to buy time so that he could figure a way to make it easier to get the herd. He just wanted to be able to get things going his own way with a minimum of effort.

It then occurred to Lassiter that if Watt could get him to commit to coming into the gang, he could run right to Morris and tell him the news. But Lassiter figured that wouldn't work, since Morris knew where Watt's interests lay. The best thing would be to play along with Watt and see what he could find out about the plan to take the herd.

"Maybe I am interested in throwing in with you," Lassiter told Watt.

Watt's eyebrows raised. "You sure?"

"Do you want to talk about this here, where everyone can listen in, or should you and I have a little discussion over in the corner?"

Watt told Johnson to sit down and the others to go

ahead and drink, while he got things settled with Lassiter. Johnson was shaking his head, but he didn't argue any longer. Watt was the one who had organized the whole thing and there would be no changing his mind.

The music in the saloon began once again and the patrons went back to drinking and gambling. Watt scowled at the saloon girl as he passed her with Lassiter. She ignored him and melted into the crowd in search of another cowhand.

Before they could begin their discussion, Lassiter and Watt both turned to see Johnson coming toward them. His face was set hard and he intended to get his concerns aired right away.

"What do you think you're doing?" Watt asked Johnson.

"I ain't letting you make all the decisions without me," Johnson told Watt. He then made a motion toward Lassiter. "That ain't fair that he should get in on this now—not after we've done all the work."

"He's already on the inside as tight as he can get," Watt explained. "He could make a lot more money working with us than getting trail wages from Ben Morris."

"What about our cut?" Johnson asked. "That makes it less for all of us if he comes in."

"Less of something is better than a whole lot of nothing," Watt reasoned.

Johnson looked at Watt again. "Are you saying this one man is going to stop us from getting that herd?"

"You shouldn't have to ask that, Johnson," Watt said smugly. "It's already happened once—just today. Or don't you remember?"

Johnson was embarrassed and angered at the same time. What Watt had just stated was true—he had

backed down from Lassiter. But he didn't want Watt
to think it was because of fear. Practical reasoning was
what had made him consider the odds. And he wanted
Watt to understand that.

"Listen," Johnson growled to Watt, "I just figured
earlier today that there was no need for gunplay over
just two hundred head when we could plan things right
and get two thousand." He motioned toward Lassiter.
"This milk-sucker here don't scare me."

Watt smiled. "Good. Then why don't you just draw
on him now and get it over with?"

Johnson started to turn and face Lassiter. Then it
occurred to Johnson that Watt was using him, making
a fool of him, and he turned again to Watt.

"So, you want me to take him out while you
watch—is that it? If I do, then I get a bigger cut of the
profits at the end of the trail."

Watt frowned. "I told you we might be able to work
with this man. Now you want to try and shoot him and
take more if you get the job done. What if you fail?
Who gets your cut then?"

"I ain't going to fail," Johnson said. "I'm going
back over with the boys for a while. Then I'll be back
to see what's happened between you two."

Johnson left without another word and it occurred
to Lassiter that the big rustler was confused. He
wanted to draw, but he didn't like the idea that Watt
was using him in some kind of game. Lassiter figured
Johnson would spend some more time drinking whiskey, then decide if he wanted a gunfight.

With Johnson finally gone, Watt looked hard at
Lassiter. He tossed down a shot of whiskey and ad-
dressed Lassiter with a little smile.

"I don't think you're even close to interested in
joining us," he told Lassiter. "You think if you can

get me to take you in, you'll get more information. That's all you want, ain't it?''

Lassiter had to give Watt credit. He had certainly been able to see that there was no reason for him to join the thieves when he had a better deal with Ben Morris. But Watt had brought the idea up and Lassiter wasn't going to let him forget that.

"So why did you ask me to join in front of your men?" Lassiter asked. "That seems kind of silly to me."

"It could work," Watt said. "If you were so inclined, it could work real well."

"Johnson wouldn't stand for it," Lassiter said. "I'd have to kill him. You know that. Are you just trying to get rid of Johnson?"

Watt blinked once and tossed down another whiskey. "It ain't none of your affair," he finally told Lassiter. "And you'd best leave Ben Morris's herd, or die with all the rest of them."

"Let's make this real short then," Lassiter said. "No, I don't intend to leave Ben Morris. But I do intend to stop you from coming after the herd. I know what you're up to now, and you'd better not try and pull it off."

"I don't think you know what we're up to," Watt hissed through his teeth. "You'd just be guessing."

Lassiter tossed down a shot and poured another. "I won't have to guess much. That girl told me a lot about what was being said over at your table."

"That girl is drunk, and crazy to boot," Watt said. "I told you that before. She don't know that country out there. She's lying."

"I'll take her word over yours any day," Lassiter said.

Watt's face reddened. His hand lowered toward his

75

gunbelt, but he restrained himself from touching the butt of his revolver.

"You haven't got a chance, Lassiter," Watt finally said. "We're getting that herd and there's nothing you can do to stop us."

Lassiter studied Watt a short while. He wondered why he was even giving Watt the consideration of telling him to back down; it would be much easier to let him come ahead and then just shoot him.

But Lassiter knew things were never that simple. If he didn't try and dissuade Watt now, Watt would come ahead with his rustlers and there would be gunplay. There was a good chance some cowhands would be hurt or killed, and that didn't need to happen. It was always better to head trouble off if possible.

But Morgan Watt was not one to be headed off easily.

"You'd just as well tell Morris to give up the herd now," Watt told Lassiter. "Make it easy instead of hard."

"Do you think myself and the Bar 9 hands are the only thing standing between you and the herd?" Lassiter asked him.

Watt nodded. "I don't know who else."

"Well, don't think I'm the only one who's onto you," Lassiter said. "A bunch of Texas Rangers came into camp tonight. They know all about you. In fact, they're staying at the herd right now. You're lucky they didn't catch you with those stolen cattle you herded in with our bunch."

Watt suddenly straightened. "What are you talking about?"

"You heard me—Texas Rangers. They're taking that bunch you stole and rebranded back to the panhandle country first thing in the morning. I'd watch myself if I were you."

Watt stared at Lassiter through eyes that were mere slits. "You're bluffing," he said. "You're just bluffing."

Lassiter grunted. "Want to take a little ride outside of town? I'll introduce you to the captain."

"I'm not going anywhere with you," Watt said.

"Have it your way," Lassiter told him. "But I'd feel obligated to warn your men, if I were you."

"I don't need to warn them about something that don't exist," Watt spat.

"Then I'll tell them," Lassiter said. He set his shot glass down and started back over for the table.

Watt went around him quickly, but saw that nothing was going to stop Lassiter. Watt went around the table and started telling the men that Lassiter would be telling them lies.

"You'll hear me out," Lassiter told them. "Anyone who wants to leave will go out dead."

Johnson had obviously been drinking heavily since he had left Lassiter and Watt to talk. Now Johnson and Watt and the others all glared at Lassiter, some of them with their hands resting below the table. But Lassiter stood back, his two big Colts within easy reach.

"We're all going to have a talk," Lassiter continued. "And anyone who doesn't remember what's said here today might have a lot of trouble with the Bar 9 outfit in the future—and with me in particular."

Watt sat back down in his chair and watched Lassiter. His face pinched with anger while Lassiter warned them all about the Texas Rangers and causing trouble with the Bar 9 herd. They all listened without so much as a word, chewing their tobacco and drinking and sizing Lassiter up.

"Just so you all know where things stand," Lassiter

concluded. "Should any of you show up out there on the trail, I won't take it as a friendly visit."

Johnson was rising from his seat again. His eyes were whiskey mean and his face was hard. He looked at Lassiter a moment and he began to grin.

"Mister, you ain't going to get a chance to see that trail ever again," he said.

9

Johnson stood in front of Lassiter, his hand close to his gun and his eyes even more determined. Suddenly everyone around noticed the situation and cowhands, gamblers and saloon girls alike moved out of the way again. This time it was for real.

Johnson was chewing furiously on a wad of tobacco he had implanted into his mouth. He squinted into Lassiter's eyes from across the table. His big frame would have been imposing to anyone but Lassiter.

"You talk mighty big, mister," he said. "And I've decided you ain't near as big as you think you are."

"Don't mess with him now," one of the others said, rising beside the cowhand and putting his hand over the man's gun. "Just lay back until the time's right."

Lassiter faced Johnson across the table, resting comfortably with his weight evenly distributed on the balls of both feet. His hands hung near the black handles of his twin Colt revolvers and he awaited Johnson's move.

Watt was watching closely, now eager to have Johnson draw on Lassiter. This would give Watt a free opportunity to see how fast Lassiter really was. It would be an indication of whether he, himself, stood a chance against this gunfighter dressed in black.

"Let it be." The rustler was still trying to persuade Johnson to leave Lassiter alone and let them handle it later.

"I don't aim to let no sidewinder just talk me down like that," Johnson said. "Once was enough. Not a second time."

Johnson went for his gun. Lassiter wasn't worried in the least, as he knew already that Johnson would have no chance. Lassiter almost leisurely pulled one of his pistols and fired before Johnson had even gotten his revolver cleared from the holster.

Lassiter hadn't called upon even half of his quickness. But to the others, the pull seemed like lightning. The blast from Lassiter's big Colt filled the room with smoke and sent Johnson tumbling backward from the table and into a heap on the floor.

The rest of the rustlers all put their hands above the table quickly, where Lassiter could see them. Some of them were trembling. None of them wanted Lassiter's gun trained on them.

But Watt remained calm. He even sported a small grin. He had watched Lassiter draw and was certain that he could pull his own revolver much faster than that.

With people gathering around the fallen cowhand, Watt considered it an inopportune time to call Lassiter. But he knew he would find the right time and beat this stranger dressed in black.

Watt got up with the other hands and talked to them for a short while. Finally, they left the saloon and he remained behind. Someone was going for the marshal, while others were checking to see if the hand was dead, which he was—completely. The bullet had blown a hole through his heart.

Watt came over to Lassiter and spoke through a smirk.

"He just about beat you. Don't tell me that's all the faster you are."

"You'd better be real certain of what you just saw," Lassiter told him. "Looks can be real deceiving."

"I don't think so," Watt said, a new confidence welling up within him. "I don't think you're all that fast, and I'm going to prove it real soon."

Watt stood and looked at Lassiter, waiting for him to say something. When Lassiter finally spoke, it was through a smile.

"If you're so sure, let's see you clear leather."

The other rustlers were hurrying for the back and Watt considered Lassiter's challenge.

"Some other time," he finally said. He started to push his way through the crowd toward the back, and turned once again. "Mark my words, I'm going to put you in a grave."

Watt moved away and was soon out the back. Lassiter turned just as the city marshal and a deputy came in. A number of people pointed to Lassiter and the two lawmen walked over, both noticeably concerned.

"I heard you were in town," the marshal told Lassiter. "You're a presence that hardly goes unnoticed."

Lassiter recognized the marshal. His name was Ben Stevens, and he'd been a deputy over in Tombstone, Arizona, for a couple of years when Lassiter had passed through quite a few years past. Lassiter had saved him from a couple of drunken gunslingers who had doubled up on him.

The deputy was quite young and seemed in awe of

Lassiter. He stood a step behind Stevens and waited to see how the marshal would handle the situation.

Stevens was relaxed now. Lassiter knew he had come into the saloon worried that there would be more shooting. But that wasn't going to happen now.

Stevens wanted to shake hands. But Lassiter knew he wouldn't do that. It wouldn't put him in good light—not when he was investigating a shooting—so he stuck to business.

"They all say he drew on you first," Stevens said, pointing to Johnson's body. "Is that the way it was?"

"I even tried to talk him out of it," Lassiter said. "Some people just don't know when to back off."

Stevens nodded, noting that the people were watching what was going on closely. A lot of them knew who Johnson was, as well as the other men who had been seated around the table. It was clear the crowd was impressed by the way Lassiter had handled the hardened rustlers singlehandedly.

"Get this man over to the undertaker," Stevens told his deputy. "We'll have him buried in the morning."

The deputy and two other men hauled Johnson out of the saloon and the music started up once again. Soon everyone was back to drinking and gambling and cavorting with the women. Stevens saw that Lassiter was looking around the saloon for other men who might be wanting to take a shot at him—especially when he wasn't looking.

"You've done in some tough ones in your time, I know," Stevens told Lassiter. "But Johnson has friends. And they'll be here to look for you, I can tell you that."

"You mean he was somebody special among thieves?" Lassiter asked.

"He controlled this whole country," Stevens said. "Now it's up for grabs."

Lassiter considered what Stevens had just told him. It made sense now to think that Watt had gotten Johnson to draw. Watt could now take over the gang and have himself a territory already.

"Tell me more about this gang of thieves Johnson was leading," Lassiter said. "I'm pretty interested."

Watt had gathered his men in the alley behind the saloon and they were now discussing what they would do. Johnson was dead and the likely replacement as leader was Watt.

The night enveloped them completely where they were and it was hard to see one another's faces—which suited most of them, as they were etched with fear now. The gunfighter dressed in black had killed Johnson without so much as a deep breath.

It scared them. Johnson had been fast with a gun. Maybe as fast as Watt at times. They had seen Johnson take men with as much ease as Lassiter had shown in killing him. And now he was gone, gunned down by a man they had never seen before.

But Watt wouldn't listen to their concern over Lassiter. He asked them instead if they were still interested in taking the Bar 9 herd. Any who wanted out were to leave right then and there. He knew he was now in charge.

No one said anything and Watt began his plan to proceed from there.

"Lassiter is going to be tied up inside for some time," Watt said. "He'll have to answer to that marshal who came in. While he's doing that, I think we'd be smart to go over to the Steer's Head and pay a visit to Ben Morris and the Bar 9 boys."

Watt's idea made sense to all of them. There was no reason they couldn't make it hard for the Bar 9 hands and make them think about wanting to get into a gunfight up the trail a ways. And it stood to reason that if they got rid of Ben Morris, the trail boss, their plan would work that much easier.

"Morris should be cleaned out by now," said the rustler who had been sitting in on the poker game with him earlier. "If I can get back into the game, maybe I can goad him into a fight and kill him. Make it look good—like he started it."

"That's what I had in mind," Watt said. "Then the rest of us can step in and punish the Bar 9 hands a little, just enough to get them to quit. The herd should be ours then."

Watt led the rustlers out of the alley and into the street. They were all confident as they made their way over to the Steer's Head and through the batwing doors. They found the establishment packed with celebrating cowhands, a lot of them Bar 9 hands spending their last few dollars before going back to the herd.

Watt spotted Morris seated at a card table and the rustler who had been playing poker with him earlier confirmed it was the same game he had left. Watt made it plain to the other rustlers they were to stay back and wait before they made any moves. The main objective was to get rid of Morris; and if he saw anybody he recognized, the plan wouldn't work.

The rustler who had been playing poker with Morris found an empty chair at the table and got back into the game. He sat across from Morris and played a few hands quietly, noting that Morris's chips were almost gone.

A saloon girl brought over a bottle of whiskey and set it down with a number of glasses. The rustler quickly poured himself a shot and downed it. Then he looked across to Morris and poured another shot.

"Want to borrow some money?" the rustler asked Morris.

Morris looked up at him, remembering him from earlier. But he did not associate him as being with Morgan Watt. Morris remembered only that this man had been playing when he had asked Lassiter for a loan. Now the man seemed to be making fun of him for some reason.

Morris looked hard at the man and shook his head.

"I'm doing fine," he said. "Keep your money, so I can win it from you."

The rustler grunted. "Don't look to me like you could win anything." He downed another shot.

Morris studied the man for a time. He couldn't figure why he was being so abrasive. Morris thought about it and poured himself a shot of whiskey. Finally, he challenged the man.

"Why don't you and I play a couple of hands between us?" Morris suggested. "We'll just play, without anyone else. Then we'll see who's winning and who's losing."

"That would be just fine," the rustler said, pouring more whiskey. He looked to the others in the game.

There were four other men at the table and they all nodded and got up. It was obvious to them that something was going on they didn't want to be part of.

The rustler shuffled the cards, smiling. Then he let Morris shuffle the cards. They cut for the first deal and Morris got a ten of hearts. The rustler showed a jack of spades, then smiled and downed another shot of whiskey.

The rustler shuffled again. He let Morris cut them and deal. Draw poker. Open on anything. Morris took his cards and moved them around in his hand, as did the rustler. Both men looked across the table at each other, studying one another hard.

Morris decided to open with a ten-dollar gold piece. The rustler threw in his ten dollars and when Morris discarded three cards, he dealt Morris three more. The rustler then took three himself and waited for Morris.

Morris opened the betting with another ten dollars and the rustler called and raised him ten. Morris nodded and called the rustler's bet and won with a pair of kings, to a pair of jacks for the rustler. The rustler downed his whiskey.

Morris smiled and raked in the money. He noted that the man he was playing didn't seem particularly bothered over losing the hand. Morris was, himself, elated. He had been losing all evening and was looking forward to getting back some of what he had lost.

The deal went to Morris and he shuffled the cards. After a moment, while everyone watched from around the table, Morris began to distribute the cards. The rustler looked at his hand and opened with a twenty-dollar gold piece. Morris considered his card and threw in his twenty.

The rustler wanted just two cards. After Morris had dealt them, he gave himself three cards. He had just gotten them into his hand when the rustler yelled from across the table.

"You cheat! You dealt from the bottom of the deck!"

Morris looked up. "What?"

"You heard me. I saw what you did."

Before Morris could react, the rustler was to his feet and was going for his gun. But Morris realized what was happening and quickly reached across the table. He grabbed the rustler's wrist and held him, then pulled himself up from his seat.

The rustler yelled and tried to get his hand free to pull his gun. But Morris held tight. With his free hand, Morris reached over and grabbed the whiskey bottle. He brought it around in a wide arc and slammed it into the side of the rustler's head.

The rustler moaned and slid to the floor, blood and whiskey coating his shirt.

The men watching all moved farther back, wondering what was going to happen next. Morris was confused, knowing he hadn't been dealing from the bottom of the deck and certain no one else had thought he was, either. But the man he had been playing was so certain of it.

Morris looked down to where the rustler still lay unconscious. He tried to understand what had made the man suddenly reappear in the game and then accuse him of cheating. But try as he might, Morris couldn't make sense of it.

Morris gathered his money up. He could see now that there was not going to be a game at this table any longer. It had all happened so fast, and so final, that everyone was still staring.

Since it had been so sudden, it hadn't interrupted what was going on in other parts of the saloon. Men were still laughing and drinking, and the music was still playing. But Morris was becoming more bothered over the incident.

A Bar 9 hand who had been close by came over and Morris told him quickly what had occurred.

"I didn't want to kill him," Morris said, accounting for the last of his winnings. "I wasn't cheating."

"I don't think anyone felt you were cheating," the cowhand told Morris. "I think you were set up."

Morris turned to him. "What do you mean?"

The cowhand was pointing to where Morgan Watt and a number of men were closing in on the table from all sides. "It looks like someone was trying to kill you and wanted to use a card game to get the job done. Now there's real trouble."

"Get the other hands over here," Morris said quickly.

But Watt and the other rustlers were almost upon Morris. Both Morris and the cowhand cupped their hands against both sides of their mouths and yelled as loud as they could.

"Bar 9! Bar 9!" they screamed into the crowd. "Bar 9, over here!"

10

OVER AT THE OTHER SALOON Lassiter was standing at the bar with the marshal, Ben Stevens, discussing the rustling problem along the trail outside of town.

"They're everywhere," Stevens was saying, sipping a whiskey with Lassiter. "They come and go here, and I just hold my breath."

"Can't you run them out of town?" Lassiter asked.

"It isn't easy to push men like that around," Stevens answered.

Lassiter nodded. He hadn't known Stevens all that well in Tombstone, but it was obvious he had been hired here more for his ability to make political decisions than for his abilities with a gun. Stevens didn't want to have to contend with a lot of shootings. But he was going to have to earn the respect of the hardcases who came into town, or see a lot of bloodshed that he couldn't stop.

"They come up from the border, sneaking behind herds and looking for travelers they can stop easily," Stevens went on. "They're getting worse all the time."

"Can't you get any help from the Rangers?" Lassiter then asked. "A group of them came into camp tonight and said they'd been trailing this bunch headed up by Johnson for a long time."

"There's not enough Rangers to keep up with them," Stevens explained. "And when they come into town here, or Fort Worth, there can be some real problems."

"Do you know of a gunman named Morgan Watt?" Lassiter then asked Stevens.

"He's kin to old John Sain," Stevens replied with a nod. "But old John's fair and Watt is as rotten as they come. Hard to imagine they're of the same blood."

Lassiter then told Stevens the story of how Watt was trying to take the herd, and how Ben Morris was having problems deciding what to do with Watt, since he was a cousin of John Sain's. Watt certainly hadn't hired on to help get the herd through, but to help Johnson and the rustlers steal the herd. And up to now Ben Morris had been forced to sit by with his hands tied.

Stevens didn't know Ben Morris, though he had heard the Bar 9 had a new trail boss. News of the main drives up the trail reached the ears of most lawmen right away, for there was bound to be some kind of trouble with each one of them. And their hands always came into town for supplies and to get themselves drunk one last time before the push up into Kansas.

Stevens did know Watt well enough to realize there had to be some kind of plan to get the herd, as Lassiter suggested in discussion, but he didn't know much about Johnson or the other rustlers who had been in the saloon.

"All I know is, you picked on a rough bunch," Stevens told Lassiter. "I'd be careful; they're quick to get around to your back."

"Well, I'm partially responsible for taking two thousand head of longhorns to Dodge City," Lassiter told him. "I'm not concerned about how rough a bunch of thieves is apt to be. I'm concerned about whether they decide to try and steal cattle from the herd. These men were making plans to do just that. It's my job to dissuade them—in any manner I deem necessary."

Stevens downed his whiskey. "All I'm saying is, don't do them all in right here in Dallas. I've got to do the paperwork."

"I have a feeling whether or not I'm in town, your paperwork is going to be a load," Lassiter told him.

Suddenly, the deputy burst through the batwing doors and hurried over to where Lassiter and Stevens leaned against the bar. Lassiter could see fear etched deep into the young lawman's eyes.

"You've got to get across the street to the Steer's Head Saloon," he said, trying to catch his breath. "Watt and those other hands are into a fight with the Bar 9 outfit. They're tearing the place apart and I can't stop them."

Lassiter and Stevens were already away from the bar, moving toward the doors. Stevens began to breathe in shallow gulps, and let Lassiter take the lead.

"I guess you were right about the paperwork," Stevens said. "Now, I've just got to stay alive to do it."

Lassiter was disgusted with himself. He felt he should have known better—that Watt would certainly try and figure a way to start trouble. He had been open enough to say that his intentions were to get the herd, any way he could.

When Lassiter broke through the doors, he found the Steer's Head a free-for-all of men fighting and knocking over chairs and tables. Morgan Watt was right in the middle of it all, hitting people with the leg of a table.

Lassiter saw Ben Morris equally as involved. His shirt was torn to ribbons and his face and neck were a mass of blood. He was defending himself against a big rustler who was trying to wrestle him to the floor. Watt, after clubbing a Bar 9 hand with a table leg, came toward Morris's back.

Lassiter started for Watt, but one of the other rustlers came at him from his left side, swinging a chair. Lassiter dodged the blow and the chair shattered into fragments of wood against the top of a table.

In one quick motion, Lassiter turned and swung hard with his right hand, slamming his fist into the rustler's face and knocking him backward into the bar, where he bounced off and slid to the floor.

Another rustler came at Lassiter and he rammed a fist into the cowhand's stomach, doubling him over. A third came at Lassiter and found his face being slammed into the top of the bar as Lassiter grabbed him by the hair and forced his head downward with tremendous force.

The rustler bounced back upward, his nose smashed flat and his face a mass of blood, then turned a half-circle and fell under a table.

Watt had already swung at Morris with the table leg, missing and hitting one of his own men, who had fallen between them. Lassiter now made his way over, but Watt saw him coming and deftly slipped away and got into a position where he could check his guns.

The marshal began to shoot into the air, demanding the brawl end. But there was so much noise and confusion that some concluded there was a gunfight starting. One of the rustlers pulled and fired point-blank at Stevens, putting a bullet through the side of his head.

The deputy drew and killed the rustler immediately, putting two bullets through his chest. Other shots erupted as both the rustlers and the Bar 9 hands pulled their guns and opened fire.

Stevens lay dead as stone on the saloon floor while the young deputy stared with his mouth open.

"You'd better start shooting rustlers," Lassiter advised. "There's no time to wonder about what just happened."

The young deputy yelled for everyone to throw down their guns. But nobody was listening. The room was filled with yelling and shooting, and everywhere was confusion.

Lassiter saw Watt with his gun pointed at him. Lassiter moved just as Watt fired, and the bullet tore into the glass behind the bar, shattering it. Watt fired twice more, wildly from the hip, and Lassiter stayed down.

Ben Morris, now standing right beside Lassiter, pulled his gun just as another rustler took aim at Lassiter. Morris fired and the rustler yelled and doubled over. Lassiter rose, thanking Morris, and looked for Watt. He wanted Watt badly, as it could end the fight. But Watt had taken cover behind a table, as everyone was doing.

The gunfire continued, sporadic and without much effect. No one wanted to show himself for very long. Lassiter waited and finally saw Watt rise and look for someone to shoot.

Lassiter could have ended it there, but the young deputy stepped in front of him and held his gun on Watt. He ordered Watt to drop the gun, and told him that he was under arrest. Watt laughed and fired two shots quickly. The young deputy groaned and slumped to the floor.

Morris then yelled for the Bar 9 hands to stay down.

There was still a lot of noise, as men and women alike were pinned down by the firing, unable to leave the saloon. Lassiter knew Watt was behind the table reloading and he decided to take a chance.

Lassiter moved from one table to another, drawing fire from some of the rustlers. Morris moved across after him, telling him to be careful and not to get himself killed.

"Why didn't you stay back where you were?" Lassiter asked him. "I think I can get Watt."

Suddenly, the rustlers opened fire on the table where Lassiter and Morris were hiding. Lassiter put chairs up behind the table to protect them as much as possible. Bullets tore splinters of wood loose and scattered debris all over the floor around them.

Finally, the barrage eased as the rustlers stopped to reload. Morris could see that he was going to be killed if they opened up again, since the section of table he had been hiding behind was almost totally shot away.

"I've got to get back with the men," he told Lassiter, and started out from the table.

"Wait!" Lassiter yelled.

But Morris was already scuttling away, and he was in danger. Watt was moving around one side of the table he had taken cover behind. Lassiter moved quickly to get into position to fire, dodging bullets from other rustlers as he pulled back the hammer on one of his revolvers.

Lassiter could see plainly that Watt had a clear shot. Lassiter fired off-handed at Watt, but not before Watt had had a chance to fire. Lassiter's bullet singed Watt's ear as Watt's gun roared and struck Morris, who had nearly made it to cover behind a nearby table.

The bullet struck Morris high in the thigh, just below the hip, and he fell heavily to the floor. Lassiter now had both pistols from their holsters and began firing wildly into the general area where Watt and the mass of rustlers were all hiding behind upturned tables.

Under Lassiter's cover, some of the Bar 9 cowhands pulled Morris out of the line of fire. Morris was squirming in pain and he was hard to handle. But they finally got him behind the heavy bar where he wouldn't be hit again.

Lassiter continued to fire his pistols, his bullets chopping holes and gouges in the tables and shattering bottles and glasses. Every now and again a rustler would yell from being hit. Already there were three of them sprawled out behind the tables.

The saloon was instantly filled with gunpowder smoke. In the thick haze, the rustlers began to run toward the back door of the saloon. Other patrons in the saloon were also running and yelling and in the noise and confusion, most of the rustlers escaped, Morgan Watt among them.

Lassiter considered it useless to try and locate Watt amidst the mass of hysteria that now filled the saloon and the darkness outside. He could do better by helping get medical attention for Ben Morris and whomever else needed it—and there were a number of men on both sides who were down.

Lassiter learned that the bartender had already gone for as many doctors as he could find. Lassiter then hurried to where the Bar 9 hands were gathered around Ben Morris. His upper left leg was soaked with blood and he was nearly unconscious from the pain. But he kept saying over and over that he would get the herd through.

"Guess I should have took your advice earlier and quit while the quitting was good," Morris remarked to Lassiter. He tried to smile through the pain. "How many men did we lose?"

"I don't know for sure," Lassiter told him. "But don't let it concern you. Just lay back and wait for the doctor."

In a short time, it was determined that three Bar 9 hands had been killed and four wounded. Luckily, none of the four had sustained serious wounds—just various flesh wounds that would pose no threat to their lives. They would need treatment, but they didn't have to worry about dying.

In the face of Stevens's death, and the death of the young deputy, there seemed to be nobody in control of things. People were still crazed with fear, unable to get themselves to believe they weren't in the middle of a gunfight any longer. Lassiter worked with some other men to get them settled down.

Finally, another deputy arrived who had come over from Fort Worth. He was younger than Stevens had been, but was more seasoned. When he learned what had happened, he organized a posse of men and rode out into the darkness.

"Go with them," Morris told Lassiter. "Hunt that snake, Watt, down and bring me back his rattles."

Lassiter wanted to go with them in the worst way, but realized Ben Morris needed his support and that the Bar 9 hands would be wanting revenge right away. It wouldn't be a good idea to go after Watt and the rustlers in the dark anyway, and there was certainly no way they could stand to lose any more men.

"Watt is going to get his when the time comes," Lassiter assured Morris. "Right now we've got you and the herd to worry about. Watt can come later."

"I want his hide," Morris said. "He doublecrossed me. I want to see him pay."

"He'll pay," Lassiter said. "Just take your time."

Lassiter discussed it with the hands and they decided to send everyone without injuries back out to the herd. Though the chance that Watt and the rustlers would try for the cattle right away was small—especially being so close to town—there was no way to really know what Watt might do. It was better to be prepared if they did come.

And with the Texas Rangers still in camp to help out, Lassiter almost hoped Watt would try to take the herd. That way he would be caught right away and save all the trouble that was sure to come up the trail.

Before long, three doctors appeared and immediately pushed past throngs of gathering onlookers to take care of the wounded. They separated and went throughout the saloon, determining the extent of injury to those down.

One of them, a small man with thinning red hair, knelt near Ben Morris. With him was a young woman with long red hair and fine features. She seemed calm and collected on the outside, but within she was certainly in turmoil.

Lassiter's first impression was that her smooth skin and soft green eyes were only masking a woman who had been through a lot and was wise to the world. It was obvious in the way she surveyed the scene without even wincing at the blood, and also how she ordered people out of the way so that the doctors could move around among the patients.

She noticed Lassiter immediately and became wary. She saw his two black-handled revolvers and the black leather. Lassiter saw her shake her head just a little and look around the room to where men were sitting up, being attended to by the doctors and others willing to help.

Lassiter knelt down beside her, where she assisted the doctor.

"No need to be afraid of me, ma'am," Lassiter told her. "I'm not as bad as all that."

She seemed surprised that he would approach her like that. Lassiter thought that perhaps she had expected that he would try to impress her with his courage.

"Whenever I see a man with two guns still standing in a place where there has been a lot of shooting, I always think that man is terribly dangerous."

"A man can be dangerous," Lassiter told her, "but that doesn't make him automatically bad."

She seemed impressed. "Perhaps you're right," she finally said. "But I'm not going to take any chances."

11

THE YOUNG WOMAN CONTINUED to help the doctor attend Morris. He had given Morris something for the pain and was now looking to Lassiter for an explanation as to why he was not back with the rest of the crowd.

"I work for him," Lassiter told the doctor, pointing to Morris. "He's the trail boss for a herd of longhorns."

"I'm afraid he won't be moving cattle for a while," the doctor said bluntly. "I can't tell how badly he's hurt, but I do know that bullet caused some damage to the hip. He'll have to be moved to my office where I can operate and take the fragments out."

Lassiter nodded. He noticed the woman studying him carefully, again wondering at his guns and who he truly was. Her gaze was stern and steady, and Lassiter knew she still didn't approve.

"Can you get some of the cowhands here to help get your trail boss over to my office?" the doctor asked impatiently.

"Give me a minute," Lassiter told the doctor. "I'll have to get the hands organized and sort everything out. Then I'll have a couple of them help me move him."

The doctor nodded and Lassiter then brought the Bar 9 hands together. He informed them of Morris's condition and put one in charge for the time being. They would return to the herd and hold the cattle until there was more news about Morris's wound. The following morning, they would bury the three hands who had been killed.

Lassiter could sense the anger welling up within all of them.

"I don't want any of you riding with the posse that deputy is organizing," Lassiter said sternly. "We're really shorthanded now and if Watt and his rustlers come for the herd, we won't be able to stop them if we don't have every available man present."

The cowhands moved out sullenly, tying the bodies of their dead comrades over their horses and heading out of town in the darkness. They all realized Lassiter was right: they couldn't do any good going after the rustlers, as their main priority was to protect the herd and be sure it got to market at Dodge City.

Lassiter kept two of them behind to help him move Morris over to the doctor's office. The other two wounded hands had already been treated by one of the doctors present. Their injuries were only slight arm wounds, but the doctor had wrapped them and had given them something to put on the wounds to prevent infection. They would return to the herd with the others and watch for trouble.

Everyone's concern now was for Ben Morris, who was in pain and in danger of passing out. But he revived when he learned he was going to be moved and cared for. Though he had been shot before, he had never sustained a wound as serious.

Lassiter helped Morris to his feet and worked to get the wounded man's left arm over his neck. One of the other hands put the remaining arm over his neck and he and Lassiter carried Morris out of the saloon and into the street.

The crowd was dispersing now, but Lassiter could see a few of them watching closely, talking about the night's events and the gunman dressed in black. Lassiter could see the young woman following behind, looking stern as she carried blood-soaked bandages back for washing, listening to all that was being said.

When they got Morris to the doctor's office, they put him on a high bed and backed away while the doctor turned up the light in a large lantern.

With the sureness of one very experienced, the woman set water to boiling and arranged surgical instruments on a small table near the bed. Lassiter noted her sure, graceful movements and her knowledge of what she was doing. She quickly had everything in order.

Then she brought out some bandages and began wrapping an arm wound sustained by one of the untreated cowhands. The doctor cared for the other, whose leg had been grazed in two places. Neither of them were even in much pain. They were worried about Morris.

But there was nothing they could do and after they had been treated, Lassiter sent them back out to the herd. He gave them instructions to send word back in to him if there was serious trouble. Meanwhile, he would stay with Morris and get him back to the herd as soon as possible.

When the cowhands had left, the doctor went to the

side of the high bed, where Morris was lying, groaning in pain.

"I'll have to ask you to help me," the doctor told Lassiter. "I'm afraid this won't be pleasant."

Lassiter knew the doctor intended to probe into Morris's hip for pieces of slug and bone fragments. The doctor wasn't sure how deep he would have to go or how badly the bone was chipped. All he knew was the work had to be done or Morris would die.

Lassiter held Morris while the doctor worked a forceps into the wound and pulled slivers of bone out. He also found the bullet, or pieces of it, scattered through the hip area. After nearly an hour of searching, he finally concluded he had done all he could.

"I'm afraid that's the extent of what I can do at this time," the doctor said. "It appears to me that the hip socket itself was just grazed by the bullet and not hit directly. Fortunate, indeed, for your friend. But nonetheless, there was damage and there still may be small bone fragments loose in the wound. Likely they will work themselves out in time."

"How long will it be until he can ride a horse?" Lassiter asked.

The doctor frowned. "I shouldn't think he should try to ride very hard, or for any distance, within at least a two- to three-week period. Maybe longer."

It was Lassiter's turn to frown. "I was hoping he could get on a horse sooner. But I guess I'll have to trail boss the herd now and let him ride in the wagon."

"You are a drover?" the doctor asked. He was looking at Lassiter's guns.

"We've got two thousand head to get to Dodge City," Lassiter replied. "This shootout tonight was the result of rustlers who want the herd."

"Did you say you were going to Dodge City?" the young woman asked, suddenly interested.

Lassiter nodded. "Yes, ma'am."

The woman thought for a moment, then asked Lassiter if he thought Morris could use a nurse to help him heal up along the way. The doctor turned to her and frowned.

Lassiter raised his eyebrows. "Well, I'm sure he could, ma'am," he finally said. "But I can't say how much we could pay you. Of course, we'd pay you what we could."

"If you would allow me passage," the young woman said, "I wouldn't want to charge anything for my services."

"That is not a good idea, Molly," the doctor spoke up.

"Allow me to introduce myself," the young woman said to Lassiter, ignoring the doctor's remark. "My name is Molly Hagan, and I came originally from Memphis to work in medicine out here on the frontier. I am trained in nursing and have had considerable experience during the war."

Lassiter then introduced himself and mentioned that he had been to Memphis on more than one occasion and had found it to be a pleasant city.

"My mother remarried after the war," Molly went on, "and she now resides in Dodge City. I have received word that she is gravely ill."

"I'm sorry to hear that," Lassiter said in consolation. "I can assure you, the trip to Dodge City will be as pleasant as I can make it."

"Just being able to get there is a pleasantry in itself." Molly said.

Lassiter nodded. "I would still want to offer you something, though. You would be doing us a favor by helping with our boss."

"Allowing me passage with you is payment

enough," she told Lassiter. "I am anxious to reach Dodge City. This is the first opportunity I've had."

"We would certainly welcome the opportunity to have you along," Lassiter said.

The doctor was clearing his throat. It was obvious to Lassiter that he was not in favor of the young lady leaving his employ to join a bunch of cowhands and a gunslinger dressed in black on the trail to Dodge City. But when he saw the look of determination in her eyes, he knew he could never win his case.

"You don't know what dangers lie out there," he told her. "Wait until an appropriate party of travelers comes along."

"What could be more appropriate, or even more safe, than a large group of men who would look out for me?" she asked the doctor. "Traveling with a party of smaller number would only make the risk that much greater."

The doctor shrugged and began his work wrapping Morris's wound. Lassiter watched while Molly helped him, her eagerness at finally getting the chance to travel to the aide of her mother showing tremendously.

When Morris was taken care of, Molly spent some time packing her belongings while Lassiter tried to assure the doctor the woman would be in good hands.

"She's right when she said that traveling with a bunch of cowhands would be the safest way for her to go," Lassiter pointed out to the doctor. "Those men will bend over backwards to see that she is safe and comfortable."

The doctor, having had a chance—albeit a short one—to see that Lassiter's character was strong and sincere, could only hope that he was telling the truth about the Bar 9 trail hands. He was aware of how most any trail hand acted when he hit the saloons and brothels, and he couldn't help worrying.

"The women in saloons and brothels expect this kind of behavior," Lassiter continued. "But when you have a lady who teaches school or is somebody other than a saloon girl, most cowhands show complete reverence. I'll bet the language out there changes a whole lot while we finish this drive."

"I can only take your word that you'll do your best to assure her safe passage," the doctor said. "After all, I am only her father, so you can see my vested interest."

"I certainly can," Lassiter said with surprise. "I hadn't any idea."

"Molly hasn't had it easy with her mother and I," the doctor stated emphatically. "You might as well know, it's no secret to me, not at this point. Her mother and I separated three years ago. And though her mother chose to live the rest of her life with someone else, I cannot deny Molly's right to be with her when she is ill."

"I'm sorry about the circumstances," Lassiter said. "But your daughter will certainly be in good hands and we'll get her to Dodge City."

"I'll arrange for a carriage and take Mr. Morris and Molly out to the herd," the doctor said. "I would imagine you would like to get back as soon as possible. And I'm certain Molly won't sleep a wink here tonight."

Lassiter nodded and the doctor left the office. Ben Morris was now lying still on the bed and he turned when he saw Lassiter walking over to him.

"How are you feeling?" Lassiter asked.

"I thought I was dead for a while," Morris answered. "All I can remember is Watt aiming at me and firing."

"You were talking for a while," Lassiter told him. "I guess you don't remember that."

"Nothing," Morris replied.

"You're not even close to dead," Lassiter assured him. "And you won't be getting any closer, unless you eat what's in the back of Whiskey's chuck wagon."

Morris frowned. "I suppose you're telling me I'll have to ride back there until I can sit a horse."

Lassiter nodded. "Two or three weeks, according to the doctor. But that's better than a grave, which is what three of the hands got."

"What about Watt?" Morris asked.

"He got away with the rest of the rustlers," Lassiter answered. "A few of them were killed, but not enough to stop them from coming at us sooner or later."

"How are we going to handle them, shorthanded like we are?" Morris asked.

"I thought I would talk to that young deputy in the morning," Lassiter said. "He ought to be back from the chase after Watt and the others. I doubt if he'll have done any good, but maybe he knows three or four good cowhands looking for work."

Morris nodded. He was grimacing from his wound. There wasn't a doubt that they would need three to four men to get the herd through.

"Hire whoever you need," Morris told Lassiter. "John Sain stands behind me, and I'll stand behind you."

The doctor drove up in the carriage. It was obvious he had been thinking more about his daughter leaving and had tried once more, unsuccessfully, to talk her out of the trip. The discussion had turned into a heated argument and Molly finally had gone into another room in tears.

The doctor paced the floor and Lassiter decided he would risk getting told it was none of his business

rather than stand by and see Molly and her father say
things to each other that they could regret.

"I don't want to speak out of turn," Lassiter told
him, "but you are both very good people and I would
hate to have you turn against one another. Maybe both
of you could ride along."

"That's not possible," the doctor said. "I have
commitments here and I cannot leave town. I'm just
worried for her safety."

"If she stays, she may always wish she had gone
with us and blame both herself and you," Lassiter
pointed out. "She might never be able to be happy
again if her mother died and she didn't get to see
her."

"Perhaps I am being selfish," the doctor concluded
after some thought. "I guess it's not my place to try
and keep her here."

The doctor then went into the other room and talked
with Molly for a time, and helped her finish her packing. When Molly was ready to go, Lassiter loaded her
things and then put one of Morris's arms around his
neck again and helped him into the passenger seat of
the buggy. Molly, wearing a split skirt, got onto a
horse the doctor had brought from the livery.

Lassiter reached into his pocket and left twenty
dollars in gold for the doctor's services and got on his
black stallion. The ride out to the herd was quiet for
the most part. It was getting close to dawn and as they
approached camp, they could hear the men on night
watch singing to the cattle. Whiskey was already up,
getting breakfast made, and when he saw Molly his
jaw dropped.

"We're replacing you," Lassiter joked.

"Suits me," Whiskey said. "Can I just ride along,
though, and enjoy the scenery?"

Lassiter introduced the doctor and Molly to the old

cook and told him about Molly's wishes to reach Dodge City and visit her ailing mother. Whiskey was impressed to hear she had been a nurse during the war and was happy to hear that she would enjoy helping him with the cooking chores in addition to taking care of Ben Morris.

Whiskey had already heard about the trouble in town from the hands. All of them were out watching herd, in case Watt and the rustlers decided to take a chance. They were all angered about what had happened and wanted to get back at Watt any way they could. The three dead drovers who had been killed in the shootout were lying at the edge of camp, wrapped in their saddle blankets, awaiting burial at sunrise.

Jack Chapman and his group of Rangers were already gone from camp. As soon as he had heard what had happened, Chapman took his men out to join the posse in search of Watt and the rustlers. Whiskey told Lassiter that Chapman would be back for the Double D 6 longhorns later.

Dr. Hagan was reluctant to leave and was considering Lassiter's offer to come along. But he finally decided that his place was in Dallas, working at his profession. To go up the trail with Molly and meet his estranged wife would only cause a lot of conflict and hardship.

Molly said goodbye to her father and though she couldn't help but show her enthusiasm at going up the trail, she shed a few tears at leaving him for the time being. She fully intended to come back and work with him in his practice, but she had to know her mother's condition.

She watched her father go and tried to tell herself it would only be a short time before she saw him again. It had been four years since she had seen him, and she had only been with him two months before learning about her mother.

Now she wanted to think the time would go quickly. But she knew better. Though Dodge City wasn't all that far away, it could prove to be an eternity on the frontier.

12

WHEN THE DOCTOR WAS GONE and the sun broke over the horizon, the hands took their three dead comrades and moved to a wooded place along the river. Whiskey drove the chuck wagon over so that Ben Morris could be there, as he was already confined to the back.

The cowhands took turns digging and soon there were three holes in the ground. From the back of the chuck wagon, Morris said a few words while the hands stood with their heads bowed and their hats in their hands. From among them came a few unashamed sniffles.

Molly stood back and allowed the cowhands their privacy. Her red hair streamed out from under a light blue bonnet, catching the glint of early sunlight. She straightened her cotton blouse and divided riding skirt, looking up the trail. Despite the solemn occasion, her eyes were as bright as the morning. She was going up the trail to see her mother.

Lassiter stood near the wagon and watched while they filled in the graves and erected three crude wooden crosses. Some of the younger cowhands hung near the graves for a time, unwilling to believe their friends had been killed—gone from their lives so suddenly and with such finality. After such a buildup, Dallas had been a bad stop.

Lassiter had gotten to know the hands very well and their death touched him as much as it did anyone else. He hated to think that it had happened to them, so young and with so much life ahead, but that was part of the frontier. Still, it was hard to take.

He talked with some of the young cowhands, encouraging them to understand that their friends would always be in their thoughts, if not there in person. It did little to console a couple of them, who wandered off and said they would catch up with the herd before noon.

Morris decided not to start the herd for a while yet—at least until the hands had had a chance to get themselves together after the burials. He was not going to get used to the back of the wagon very easily. He couldn't picture himself lying down while everyone else was on horseback, doing the work he had been hired to oversee.

To a great degree, Morris felt responsible for all that had happened. He was certain that if he had listened to Lassiter and had quit gambling, everyone would have returned to the herd and they would be a solid unit headed up the trail toward Dodge City.

While Morris looked out the back of the chuck wagon and relived the night in his mind, Lassiter stood and talked to him for a while. Lassiter reminded him that Watt and the rustlers had planned to hit the herd sooner or later and that after the fight in the Steer's Head Saloon, they might be more reluctant to try.

"They'll come at us again," Morris said emphatically. "You know that and I know that. You're just trying to make me feel better—to ease my guilt some. But things always get screwed up when I start gambling.''

"Taking this herd up the trail is a gamble," Lassiter pointed out. "Maybe you should change your attitude about the word 'gambling' and refer to it instead as a 'challenge.' ''

Morris shrugged. "All I know is, three of my men are dead and four others won't be up to top speed for at least a week. If Watt and his rustlers show up before then, I don't know what will happen."

"I have yet to go back into town and pick up some more hands," Lassiter said. "Don't give up yet. We'll get this herd through."

Lassiter walked away from Morris and toward his horse. It wouldn't ordinarily be difficult to hire hands for a cattle drive, but Lassiter intended to tell them there would certainly be real trouble with a gang of rustlers bent on getting the herd. Cowhands always expected trouble and rarely shied away from it. But there could be some who wouldn't want to ride into a nest of hornets.

Molly was putting her things into the wagon. She had been watching Lassiter while he talked to Morris and now as he walked toward his horse. Her look was one of curiosity.

It was obvious to Lassiter that Molly was still intrigued with him and was wondering what he was all about—a man dressed in black leather who wore two matching pistols, yet did not like to see people die.

Lassiter purposely led his horse by her before he mounted up for the ride back into town. He stopped in front of her and helped her load one of her bags into the wagon.

"I hope you don't have to watch us bury any more

men," Lassiter told her. "But I know everything won't be just green fields and clear water."

"I can handle it, Mr. Lassiter," she said softly. "Believe me, I'm ready for anything to get up to Dodge City."

"It will be good to have you helping with Morris," Lassiter said, hoisting another bag up. "I hope you can help him through this by talking to him a little. He thinks it's all his fault."

"I'm certain I can help," she said confidently. "The war taught me a lot about men and violence, and the continual turmoil that seems to exist within the male mind."

Lassiter raised his eyebrows. "You've made some acute observations, no doubt. Do you think *all* men live by the gun?"

"It is my opinion that the men who don't live by the gun do so only because they don't feel they can measure up to the ones that do. Yes, all men are terribly violent within. I believe they're born that way."

Lassiter gave another faint nod and turned for his horse. He noted that Molly had reached into her traveling bag and was checking the action on a .44 caliber Colt Dragoon.

She caught Lassiter staring.

"Is something the matter?"

"That's an awful big pistol, ma'am. There are others a lot smaller, easier to handle."

"But likely not as effective," she said. "It might take two hands and a deep breath, Mr. Lassiter, but I can fire this weapon. And I can be accurate with it, as well."

"I believe you," Lassiter told her, mounting his black stallion. "Let's hope you don't have to show me."

"Let's hope not," Molly said, lowering the big pistol back into her bag and brushing strands of red hair from in front of her eyes. "But we still have a long ways to go to Dodge City."

Watt led the rustlers into the heavy thicket of mesquite and dismounted, grabbing his rifle from its sheath. Roused from sleep, jays squawked from the branches, flitting from one thorny branch to another. The sun would soon be topping the horizon, as a crack of gray was flashing into the sky. But the thought of sunlight only made Watt more nervous.

Just out from their position in the mesquite, Watt could see riders fanning out in two directions through the dawn shadows. They had to be Texas Rangers.

It had been a running fight with the posse and the Texas Rangers ever since the sun had come up. But after trading shots for an hour, it had appeared that both the Rangers and the posse had turned back.

But now Watt knew differently. It was most certainly the Texas Rangers who were still on their trail.

Watt knew well how the Rangers operated: if they were sustaining losses coming head on, they sought some other means of reaching their goal. In this case it had been to drop back and travel quietly, and hope for a chance to strike when surprise was on their side.

Watt wasn't going to fall for it—not after his experiences with Rangers down on the border. If he wasn't mistaken, the same captain who had charged into a bunch he had been working with down there was now on his trail up here. Chapman was his name. Tough. Unwilling to quit.

But he would have to quit this time, Watt vowed. He had learned Chapman's tricks down on the Rio Grande and this time he would use the same trick against Chapman.

But he couldn't afford to lose any more men in doing it.

Watt's gang was now down to just twelve men. That was much fewer than had started the evening, and a lot of them had fallen to the gunfighter, Lassiter.

Five, in fact, had been the count. Fifteen of the twenty had left the Steer's Head in a rush after the shoot-out, but three had fallen to the Texas Rangers and the posse in the running fight after leaving Dallas. And it had happened because Watt had been careless.

Watt didn't want to think about it. But the fact of the matter was, he had made a mistake. They had gotten a good head start out of town and after an hour, he had concluded no one was coming after them. He had decided to slow the pace down to a walk, to save the horses. Then he had mistakenly let the horses drink too much at a stream crossing.

Before long they had heard the sounds of running horses behind them. Their horses had been too filled with water and even the spurs and the shooting couldn't get them up to top speed. The Rangers and the posse had caught up to them in the darkness. That's how they had lost the three men.

But Watt and the others had opened fire in the dark and there had been men yelling and cursing among the rangers and the posse. In fact, the posse had given up. But not the Rangers.

Now Watt looked out into the approaching sunlight to try and see where the riders had vanished. The other rustlers were just as worried.

"My God, we ain't shook them yet?" one of the rustlers remarked.

Another one of them laughed nervously. "They'd be crazy to come in here after us."

"Just be ready to shoot when I give the word," Watt said. He held his rifle with twitching fingers and peered out into the early light.

"Maybe they're circling around behind us," one of them speculated.

"Hell, I know that!" Watt hissed again. "I want you all to look and quit talkin'. That's what I want."

Watt then looked from man to man. He fingered the notch in his ear where Lassiter's bullet had creased him and he cursed under his breath. It was tender and it would remain that way for a number of days—a reminder that he had someone to kill.

"That black-dressed gunman ain't nobody to fool with, is he," one of the rustlers said, remembering the shoot-out in the Steer's Head saloon.

"He ain't nobody," Watt said quickly. "His time will come. We've got to stop these Rangers first."

Watt told the men to gather wood and start a fire in a little open spot where a trail led down to the water. He explained that maybe the Rangers would think they hadn't been seen and would come into camp to make the arrests. Then they could get the drop on the Rangers.

When the fire was built, Watt had the rustlers spread out and hide a good distance back from the fire. The brush was thick and the fire was impossible to see unless you walked right out into the open. Watt considered that Chapman and the others might just do that.

Watt and the other rustlers didn't have long to wait, as they soon heard the crackle of wood being broken underfoot. Only an Indian could walk through the brush and not make a sound. Boots were not made for soft walking.

Watt nodded to himself as a number of men came into view, spread out throughout the brush. They had their rifles ready and were moving slowly, deliberately, but were unaware that Watt and the other rustlers were just waiting.

When Watt began firing, the others opened up, too. Rangers yelled and fell in the thicket. Though the sun was already up, it was impossible to see their faces. But when the shooting was over and the surviving Rangers had managed to escape, Watt found one man's body that made him smile.

"Chapman," he told the others. "Can you beat that? We got Chapman himself."

"You outsmarted him with his own trick," one of the rustlers smirked. "That's mighty fine."

Watt looked around and made sure they hadn't lost anyone in the shooting. Everyone was safe, not even a scratch from the mesquite.

They had gotten rid of the Rangers, but that didn't solve the problem of how they were going to get the herd from Lassiter and Ben Morris. Watt wondered what was happening with the herd and if Morris was still alive. He knew he had wounded Morris badly, but he wasn't sure if the wound had been mortal. And even if Morris had died, there was still the other Bar 9 cowhands to contend with. And Lassiter.

"We're free to go after the herd, but what we goin' to do about the men we lost to that gunfighter?" one rustler asked Watt. "And the others we lost to them Rangers and the posse?"

"We'll have to make do," Watt said. "That just means more for us when we get the herd. That's all."

"It ain't that simple," the rustler pointed out. "We've still got to go through Injun country to get to the Canadian. Words out that Quanah Parker and them renegade Comanches are comin' out of the panhandle country and butcherin' people right and left wherever they go. There ain't enough soldiers at either Fort Sill or Camp Supply to stop them."

"What does that have to do with us?" Watt asked.

"Can't you see, we might run into them. How we goin' to get by them?"

"They've mostly been after buffalo hunters," Watt pointed out. "They look for them mostly."

"Yeah, well they ain't agin killin' us, if they took the notion," the rustler aruged. "We ain't got enough men to stand off a big war party."

Watt nodded and began considering their problem. But he realized Lassiter and Ben Morris would face the same situation. And if they took the herd far enough west toward the panhandle country to expose them to the Comanches, they would certainly have Indian problems.

Watt reasoned if he could figure a plan to get Morris or whoever was in charge to move the herd over far enough, maybe the Indians would help them get rid of the cowhands and make it easier to take the herd.

"So what do you figure we should do?" the rustler insisted. "I ain't up to havin' my scalp took by no Comanche."

As Watt looked down at Chapman's body, he thought of the Comanches and an idea came to mind.

He quickly began to rifle Chapman's clothes for money and valuables, and for his identification as well. He told the others to look carefully on the other fallen Rangers for papers or badges, or anything that identified them as lawmen.

"I think we can maybe pull another little trick to get that herd over west, where the Comanches will help us instead of hurt us," Watt said with a laugh.

He explained to the others that three of the gang

should take the clothes from dead Rangers, along with the identification, and ride to the herd and set a trap. They would show their identification and tell Morris or whoever was in charge that Chapman and the rest of their company had been killed by Comanches, and that the herd should move west to avoid trouble.

Watt then explained that whoever volunteered to do this would receive an extra fifty dollars in gold when the cattle were sold.

"They're apt to recognize us, ain' they?" one of the rustlers asked.

Watt shook his head. "Hell, no. There was too much gunsmoke in that saloon last night for anyone to see anybody clearly. They'll just hear what you've got to say and then you can lead them into the Comanches."

Five of the rustlers insisted on going, and Watt told them to settle it by cutting cards. The men then sat around the open area where they had built the fire and each of the five pulled from a deck to see who would go.

When three men were selected, Watt nodded and watched them take clothes from three of the dead Rangers and wash the blood from them in a nearby creek. The men dressed and all decided to get some sleep before enacting their plan. There was no big hurry until they got farther north past the Red River.

As he lay out his bedroll in the shade, Watt smiled to himself. He was confident the plan would work. It would stand to reason that the Rangers had chased rustlers up the trail and that Comanches had done them in. And it would also make sense that the surviving Rangers would try and find a bunch of cowhands driving a herd to throw in with for safety.

He could see himself counting the gold already, and spending it in the best spots in Dodge City. He would have the papers that said he was the trail boss for the Bar 9 outfit and Ben Morris would have nothing.

And that gunfighter, Lassiter would be dead. That's what Watt thought about mostly—seeing Lassiter dead. There wasn't anything in this world he wanted more, and he would work until that happened.

13

LASSITER RETURNED FROM DALLAS with four new hands. Three of them had worked for the Bar 9 at one time or another in the past and were eager to ride for the outfit again. It didn't seem to bother them that the danger of rustlers was imminent with this herd in particular; they had been fighting rustlers with every job they had taken for the past five years.

While back in Dallas, Lassiter had taken the time to wire a message to John Sain at Bar 9 headquarters, in behalf of Ben Morris. He wanted John Sain to know what his cousin, Morgan Watt, was up to and not to be surprised if he got word that Watt had been placed in a pine box.

Lassiter had also talked with the young deputy who had taken the posse out after Watt and the rustlers. The deputy had been tired and frustrated, and Lassiter had been able to tell he had met with no success in stopping Watt and the others.

The young deputy had told Lassiter that he had brought the posse back after a running gunfight on horseback that had cost him five men. But the Rangers had stayed out. He had told Lassiter he could only hope that the Rangers got Watt and the others—or the trail to Dodge City for the Bar 9 herd was going to be a rough one.

Lassiter brought the new cowhands and the news back to the herd. Everyone had expected Watt and the rustlers to get away. In fact, it was a surprise to learn that the posse and the Rangers had both caught up with them. Lassiter concluded that Watt had likely thought he was not being followed and had been caught by surprise.

But there was the herd to worry about now, and the trail to Dodge City would be filled with enough problems besides Morgan Watt and his gang of rustlers.

The herd moved out and left the Trinity and the bad memories behind. Over the next few days, Lassiter essentially took over Ben Morris's duties as trail boss, consulting often with Morris as he discussed matters from the back of the wagon. Morris was anxious and was hard to keep confined. He was not happy with his situation, but he considered himself extremely lucky to be alive.

Within the week, the cowhands had settled into the new routine of working harder together in order to keep the herd moving at a steady pace and still keep the longhorns from losing any weight. They had nearly two month's travel yet to Dodge City, barring any serious problems, and the faster they moved, the faster they could sell the cattle and forget the worry over Morgan Watt.

Everyone tried to forget Watt and take things day by day. During Lassiter's frequent scouting trips ahead and around the herd, he left different men in charge, to divide up the responsibilities and make every man feel important in the effort to get the herd up the trail.

This helped unite all of them into a stronger unit. No one felt left out and no one climbed higher in rank over the others. Lassiter wanted to keep things—as much as possible—the same as before the fateful night in Dallas. Then when Watt came, and he certainly would, everyone would be ready to stay together.

The herd moved north along the trail, making nearly twenty miles during each stretch between dawn and nightfall. There was no sign of Watt and the rustlers and though Lassiter scouted a good deal out from the herd each day, he could find no fresh sign of anybody having camped close.

Possibly the Rangers had succeeded in getting Watt and the others. Lassiter hoped that was the case, though he sensed that Watt knew too many tricks from his killing days on the southern border to let anyone really get the drop on him.

Watt couldn't be forgotten or taken for granted, and every hand remained wary day and night. The guard was always doubled during darkness hours and each man—whether asleep or awake—kept himself ready for the sound of alarm and the need to hurry into the saddle and save the herd from whomever or whatever might come.

Molly Hagan was soon the favorite of all among the drovers. She didn't put on airs and she didn't want anyone to think she was above talking with the men. During the day, she rode with the drovers and began to learn about pushing cattle up a trail. Though it was hot and dusty work, she enjoyed it and found herself looking forward to each new day.

Molly proved to be what Ben Morris needed to keep him quiet and allow his wound to heal properly. She dressed his hip twice daily and his condition improved markedly in just the first week. He had shaped a cane for himself from a big chunk of Palo Verde and hobbled around camp, making himself do whatever he could to help.

But Molly was strict about how active he was allowed to be and kept him a good distance away from his horse. That was the hardest part for Ben Morris—not being able to ride. His life depended on his ability to use a horse. To be out of the saddle for so long was driving him crazy.

Morris took a lot of kidding from the hands about being bedridden for the most part inside a wagon. They asked him what it was like to sleep all day and then try to pester Molly all night. They all realized she slept by herself out on the ground, but they accused Morris of making a lot of noise every time he tried to sneak out of the wagon.

One of the hands spent three nights carving a surprise for Morris from two small pieces of mesquite wood. When the hand was finished with his carving, all the hands gathered around the chuck wagon just before an evening meal to see Morris get the surprise. Everyone laughed and hooted when Morris was presented with a pair of darning needles.

"Me and all the boys thought you'd like to have something to do with your hands," the cowpuncher laughingly told Morris. "Maybe you've found your real lot in life."

Whiskey chewed on a piece of root and remarked that he had often noticed Morris in the back of the wagon, rummaging through the supplies looking for twine to knit with.

Morris took the joke good-naturedly and pointed out that he should darn a pair of new socks for every man on the drive, but that it still might not rid the camp of the smell when everyone took off their boots.

Molly stood with Lassiter and laughed with everyone. She had fallen into helping with Whiskey's cooking chores and the food had improved markedly.
Though Whiskey wasn't about to admit it to anyone,
Molly had taught him some easy ways to spice up the
flavor of the bland offerings of plain beef and beans
and occasional baking powder biscuits.

She had learned while working as a nurse on the
battlefields of both the North and the South that food
and the way it tastes can be a gigantic morale booster.
She was of the opinion that various battles were won
and lost merely by the way the men were fed and how
well.

Molly had told Lassiter more than once when he
had asked during the meals that it wasn't necessarily
the amount of food that men were fed, but the quality
and the taste. She showed Lassiter how she could
improve the flavor of almost anything by cooking it
over various woods and throwing in natural spices that
existed within native plants growing in the area.

This had actually impressed Whiskey more than he
wanted to admit. Though he had been chewing various
roots for a lot of years, he hadn't learned the wild
plants that could be used as seasonings in foods. He
had been content merely to chew and spit.

While Ben Morris joked with the cowhands about
the darning needles he had been given, Lassiter ac-
companied Molly on a walk outside of camp. She was
gathering mesquite wood and picking various plants
she was going to give to Whiskey to put into the
morning meal.

She was mainly looking for plants of wild mint and
rhubarb that she knew would be growing near the
springs. She was going to keep her eyes open for
various other plants as well, and was willing to teach
Lassiter what she could.

They had been lucky enough to find this spot and had stopped for the night because of the good grass. It was getting late in the evening when they began their walk and Molly was anxious to collect as much of everything she could find before it got dark. If she waited until morning, there would be very little time to find anything and collect it before the herd started once again.

At the lower end of the spring, where it spread into a large marshy area, Molly found a number of plants she knew she wouldn't see the rest of the trip. Lassiter helped her collect them and place them in flour sacks she had made small holes in for aeration.

"This is fortunate we have stopped here," she said with a lilt in her voice. "Now the men will be anxious to eat and there won't be as much grumbling."

Lassiter had to laugh. "You think they grumble now? Compared to what there was before you came along, everyone is real quiet now."

Molly smiled. "They sound rather vehement against Wiskey at times. I guess they just like to tease him."

"That's basically their only means of entertainment," Lassiter explained. "If they couldn't rankle the cook, or one another at times, they would all go crazy."

"They seem to be a good group in general," Molly then remarked. "But a lot of them are awfully young for such a journey."

"It seems everyone has to start the hard part of life too young," Lassiter said in a low tone. "You can't get away from it."

Molly stopped her plant collecting and looked up into Lassiter's eyes. She looked at him for a time, as if to convince herself for sure that she wasn't making a mistake in her assessment of him.

"During the war, I was around a lot of men," she

finally said. "And I nearly married twice. But I've never known anyone like you."

"I'm not so special," Lassiter said.

"I didn't say you were special. I said you were different. You can preserve life as easily as you can take it. In fact, it seems to me you work harder to preserve it. Why wear the two pistols? It only marks you."

"I'm marked," Lassiter replied. "That's the way it is, and I can't change it."

"Have you ever tried?"

"I tried, yes. More than once."

When Lassiter said no more, Molly pushed him.

"Tell me about it."

Lassiter took a deep breath. "The first time, I was working for a cattle company in Colorado Territory. Somebody from Utah recognized me and tried to shoot me in my sleep. He would have told everybody he had faced me down, but it's easier to shoot a man in the back and make the story up later."

"Did you have to kill him?" Molly asked.

"It was either that or die myself. I had to dodge his bullets until he shot the gun empty. Then I took it away from him and he came at me with a knife."

Molly nodded and waited for him to tell her about the second time.

"Then I got it into my head again that I wanted to get rid of these guns, for good. But once again someone from somewhere knew me and tried to kill me anyway. He nearly got the job done and would have, if it hadn't been for a lady like you."

"A lady like me?" Molly asked. After she had spoken, she knew what he meant and didn't want him to go on.

"No, you wanted to hear it," Lassiter told her. "We were going to be married. Instead, he shot her to get to me. That didn't have to happen as far as I'm concerned. I gave him his chance to face me down and emptied both guns into him. And ever since then I've decided I've got to face the rest of my life being who I've always been—good or bad, I can't escape it.''

Molly looked at him for a time again. She finally nodded slowly to herself.

"Good, not bad," she said. "I know you're good."

"It's a life always looking behind you," Lassiter said. "Always reading what's in a man's eyes when he talks to you. You listen to the tone of his voice, no matter what he's telling you, and you look in his eyes. That's how I stay alive."

"I've had to use my big pistol more than once," Molly confessed. "It makes me sick to remember it, but I had no choice."

"Sometimes there is no other choice," Lassiter said with a nod. "If there is, I'll take it. If there isn't, I just do what I have to do."

"Do you ever forsee yourself settling down?" Molly then asked.

"I don't know how I could ever do that," Lassiter replied. "There's always someone who wants a chance at me. And I'll never allow someone to die again, just because some killer is looking for a reputation."

"I do hope you find peace one of these days," Molly said, moving in closer to him. "You deserve it."

Lassiter took her in his arms, then leaned over and kissed her. She responded by pulling him closer to her and holding him tightly. Then she suddenly backed away.

"What in the world am I doing?" she asked herself.

"I didn't mean to upset you," Lassiter said.

Molly looked at him and in the twilight, her blue

eyes were soft. But she was determined to hold onto herself.

"We shouldn't have come out here together," she said honestly. "I knew my feelings would get the best of me."

"Don't blame yourself for your feelings," Lassiter told her. "I have feelings as well. Maybe when we both have the same feelings, they get stronger within each of us."

"I have no doubt about that," Molly said, picking up her sacks of plants. "And if I stay a moment longer, I won't be able to control myself."

Lassiter watched her hurry away from him, through the shadows of twilight, back toward camp. He had known upon first meeting her that she was a special woman. But he hadn't known until this evening just how special.

14

RED RIVER STRETCHED ACROSS the northern boundary of Texas, a twisting formation of swirling water that had the reputation of dragging men and horses to the bottom. It was wide and very deep in places. And it was the concern of every Bar 9 cowhand as they got their horses ready for the day's drive.

They would reach the river in mid-afternoon. Lassiter rode ahead to find a good crossing and rode back to report that the water was down. The hands all cheered and the remainder of the drive to the river was spent joking instead of worrying.

Ben Morris had been in the saddle for small stretches at a time for the last two days. Molly hadn't allowed him any more time than what she considered safe for his healing hip. He didn't like it, but he had learned to tolerate her nursing him.

Morris had long since learned not to argue with Molly, for she had told him more than once that she felt responsible for his recovery—obviously more so than him—and didn't intend to see his improvement go to waste just so he could sit in a saddle. There was still a lot of country to cross to reach Dodge City, and he would get enough of the saddle again once the wound healed sufficiently.

The sun crossed overhead in the sky and the herd stretched out for nearly a mile. Toward mid-afternoon, the bluffs of the river rose ahead and Morris had the hands bunch the cattle. They were watered at a small tributary stream before starting into the main channel, making it easier to get them across and keep them from stalling in the current to drink.

Lassiter sat his black stallion and watched the heard begin the crossing. The water was down and moving through several small channels. Though the current was moving much slower than it had been not many days earlier, there was still a lot of red silt coloring the flow.

In addition, accumulations of fallen trees on the sandbars and other debris piled along both banks indicated that the river had been swollen much higher for a good long time. Anyone who had tried to cross before now would have no doubt lost men and stock both.

The herd crossed at a good pace, taking the entire width of the channel without stopping even for a short time. Though he wanted in the worst way to cross with Lassiter and the other hands, Molly insisted that Morris ride in the chuck wagon and not take a chance on having an accident on his horse.

Across the river from Texas was new territory. The north bank of the river marked the Indian lands, and stretched northward into a vast domain of primitive country as far as the eye could see, and a flowing sea of green showed itself across the endless plains.

The trail followed a divide between the Salt Fork and the North Fork of Red River. Not far to the east was the reservation—where the Comanche shared what little there was with the Kiowa-Apache and Kiowa tribes. Lassiter knew that the Comanches especially were waging all-out war against the whites, and the buffalo hunters in particular, and that there had been reports of raids in the area.

They were getting into the most dangerous part of the drive. But once past this area, the drive to Dodge City would be relatively easy.

The herd was allowed to graze while Whiskey and Molly fixed the meal for the evening. It was earlier than usual, but the hands were tired from pushing so hard for so long, and they welcomed the chance to stop early and let the herd fill up before moving on at first light.

Lassiter rode to the top of a hill with Molly. Far in the distance was a series of black spots that Lassiter knew to be buffalo. They were being slaughtered by the thousands now and their numbers were dwindling far more rapidly than anyone had ever expected.

The days of seeing them grazing in herds that blackened the plains for endless miles was a thing of the past. That was likely the main reason the Comanche were depredating every buffalo hunter's camp and white settlement they could.

Lassiter sat his horse and looked out for a time, seeing the distance as endless toward the north. Molly seemed to be looking at something different, something that made her reflect on what used to be.

"I have a strange feeling about this land ahead of us," Molly told Lassiter. "It seems so vast and empty. But once it was filled with life, and now it's sad."

"What do you mean?" Lassiter asked. "The land itself is sad?"

"Yes. The very being of the ground here and everything that lives here is sad. You can feel that these plains are facing the end of their existence as we see it now."

Lassiter couldn't help but think Molly was seeing change coming, even to this remote region that had never before been interrupted by anything that resembled civilization. Now she was saying that civilization was coming to destroy what they were looking at—whatever would be left after the buffalo hunters were gone.

"How can you feel that just from sitting here and looking out there?" Lassiter asked. He was well aware that among Indian peoples, there were women as well as men who could foretell the future. They could see it in their minds. But Molly was talking about feeling it.

They rode back down to camp and Molly went to gather more plants to use in cooking. Lassiter watched the hands play cards and tell stories about other drives through this segment of the trail. As he watched them, he wondered what they would encounter here and how it would affect them.

Like Molly, he had a feeling that things were going to change. But unlike her sense of total change in the future, his feeling was of something happening very soon.

Watt and the rustlers swam their horses across the lowered flows of Red River and stopped for a time on the north side. They had been following the herd at a distance of some ten to twelve miles, so they wouldn't be detected. Now, as they entered Indian lands, they decided to talk again about how they would work to get the herd.

They had crossed some five miles upriver from where the herd had forded and Watt knew there was no need to be in a big hurry just yet. It was likely the herd would be allowed to graze for at least a day, to build up strength and put on weight for the drive through the open plains toward Dodge City.

Watt saw this as a good opportunity to eat a full meal and rest. What was behind had been rough, but what lay ahead would be rougher.

But there would be no fire. Some of the men complained and Watt pointed out that Lassiter would certainly be on the lookout for Indians. If he saw smoke and then later watched three men riding into camp, asserting to be Texas Rangers, the first thing he would ask himself would be: Who's smoke was that? You don't build fires in hostile Indian country if there are just three of you.

The rustlers finally conceded to eating cold beans, with the promise from Watt that he would buy them each a bottle of whiskey and a steak when they sold the herd at Dodge City. He realized it was important to keep them looking forward to something; otherwise this most important part of the plan could go wrong very easily.

The day passed slowly and the men became restless and uneasy. They talked endlessly about the plan to take the herd—the idea of posing as Texas Rangers. It seemed logical that the survivors of an Indian attack would be looking for the first large group of men to join up with.

Everyone was convinced it would work, and everyone wanted to go right ahead with it. One of the men who had cut cards and won the right to pose as a Texas Ranger was insistent that they begin their plan right then. In fact, he soon got pushy about it.

His name was Markley. He was of medium height and build and very dark complected. He had a habit of talking a lot about women and by now the other rustlers had become accustomed to him, and rarely took him seriously.

Markley was adamant about getting started. He crowded in next to Watt while they sat eating.

"The sooner we get this underway, the sooner we get that herd," he told Watt.

"Why don't you consider letting those cowhands drive that herd a ways for us first?" Watt asked. "It's not going to be easy getting through this country with just a dozen of us."

The other two who would go into the camp as surviving rangers were a small man named Bauer and a young, tall rustler named Skip. They sided with Markley.

"The longer we wait, the more chance there'll be something happen that we don't get the herd," Bauer argued. "There ain't no other herds and no Injuns around now. Nothin' is around to interfere. I say let's do it."

Watt started to argue again, but the other rustlers sided with the three and spoke up to override anything Watt had to say. He was tired of being around impatient men; but after being on the trail as long as they had, the rustlers wanted to get the herd and go north as quickly as possible.

Watt finally gave in and told them to go ahead, if that's what they wanted. But he warned them that if they weren't convincing to the Bar 9 cowhands—especially the gunfighter, Lassiter—they could be in for real trouble.

"You had just better figure that to get the job done, you've got to *act* like Texas Rangers," Watt told the three. "Have any of you thought about that at all?"

"What is there to that?" Markley asked. "How are they any different than anybody else?"

Watt snorted. "Did you ever stop to think they're

trained men and that they can't just be like everybody else? They've learned to be real quiet and to look everyone over real careful."

"We can be quiet-like," Bauer said without hesitation. "We don't want to talk much anyway. Just say what happened to our unit and that we think the herd ought to turn west a ways."

"There's more to it than that," Watt argued. "Especially if you're going to fool Lassiter."

"He ain't no Texas Ranger," Markley argued.

"He might not be," Watt said, losing patience. "But he *acts* like one. You've got to be like him. You can't be anxious when you get into their camp. You've got to hold back some."

"How do you mean?" Bauer asked.

Watt hesitated so they would all listen closely. "If I was a ranger and I'd gotten my unit butchered by a bunch of Comanches, I'd come into camp damn angry—but with my head down. You see, rangers ain't supposed to lose."

"You mean, we shouldn't be too eager to just tell them to get their cattle moved away from the Injuns?" Markley asked.

"Now you're starting to get the idea," Watt told them. "Just say there was a bunch of Injuns up north that killed all of your unit but you three. Then say you wouldn't be caught up there with a whole army of men—them Injuns are that mean."

"We'll play it smart," Markley promised. "We'll just say there ain't no way a herd can get by them Comanches."

Watt nodded. "Just say that and then tell them you figure to go on west, just the three of you, the next morning. That way, Morris—if he's still alive—and that gunman, Lassiter, will come up with the idea to skirt around the area themselves."

The youngest of the three, the tall one named Skip, hadn't spoken yet. But now he wondered if there was going to be a chance that they could get themselves killed by Comanches either going or coming from the herd.

"I ain't sure that just the three of us riding alone is very smart," he contended.

Watt shrugged. "You want to give up your right to the bonus to someone else? Have them cut the cards again to see who takes your place?"

Skip thought about it. Finally he shook his head.

"No. I'll go along."

"Good," Watt said. "Be ready at first light."

15

IN LATE AFTERNOON of the second day past Red River, Lassiter and Morris rode to the top of a small rise and looked down into the Washita. There was still a lot of grass available and the herd was well-rested from the stop two days before.

Lassiter sat his horse and watched the herd cross the river with ease. Morris sat his horse next to Lassiter's and they shared a discussion about the drive thus far. Morris was now riding more and more and he was happy to be back working. He felt like part of the Bar 9 outfit once again.

They rode down to the river's edge and studied the current. Morris was going to be riding through water for the first time since the saloon shoot-out.

"I didn't feel like much more than an old woman there for a while," Morris commented. "I started looking at those darning needles real hard."

"Maybe you could learn to knit on horseback," Lassiter suggested.

Lassiter eased his black stallion into the current and

138

watched Morris closely as he rode alongside on his own horse. It was obvious that Morris's leg was bothering him some, but not enough to make him say anything. It would take a lot of pain to make Morris want to get down from the saddle.

Molly didn't seem to be paying as much attention to her duties as a nurse now. For some reason, she didn't seem to care like she did. She didn't seem to care about much of anything, it seemed.

As much as Morris was improving, Molly seemed to be someone different from that pretty redheaded lady who had joined the herd to go to Dodge City and see her mother. She had become withdrawn since her talk with Lassiter while gathering plants. She wasn't as jovial as she had been and she didn't make herself as available to the hands as she had before. In fact, she hadn't spoken once to Lassiter since that night.

A marked change had come over her and Lassiter felt he was to blame.

The herd crossed with no trouble and as the cattle spread out to graze, the hands gathered to talk. Lassiter left Morris as he chatted with some of the hands and rode over to where Molly was just riding up from the river onto the bank.

She saw him coming and tried to ride past him. But he grabbed her horse's reins.

"What's happening to you?" Lassiter demanded. "You've got everyone worried."

"It's my own affair," she said bluntly.

"No, it's everyone's affair," Lassiter argued. "The hands have all taken a special liking to you and they're worried. Frankly, so am I. And I wonder if I didn't cause it."

Molly looked hard at Lassiter. "Why would you think you caused anything?"

"The other night, collecting plants. I maybe shouldn't have wanted you like I did."

"But you didn't do anything wrong."

"I don't know if I did or not. I just felt like you had something happen inside of you."

Molly was silent a moment. "I did," she finally admitted.

"Well, fix it," Lassiter told her. "We all want the old Molly back."

For the first time in two days, she smiled.

"I didn't think I'd ever see you do that again," Lassiter told her. "Is it something I said or did?"

"No, no, don't blame yourself," Molly insisted. "I've just had to come to terms with myself on a few things, that's all."

"If there's anything I can do to help . . ."

"Thank you, Mr. Lassiter," Molly said with a smile. "But there's nothing you can really do. But what you just said, is it really true? Do you and the men think that much of me?"

"Of course we do," Lassiter said. "You should know that. There isn't anyone else like you, so just remember that."

"I have to thank you for making me come to some realizations," Molly said after another short silence. "You brought something back to me, something I've been holding deep within me. You can see that and you want me to get back to my old self. Is that it?"

Lassiter nodded. "We all do. We've been concerned that you haven't been as happy as you were when you joined the drive at the Trinity."

"I am now," she said. "After talking with you the other night, and just now, I see that I've got to live my life for the future and not the past." She was pointing to the logs and driftwood that were lodged on the sandbars and along the river's edge. "All this debris gets washed away and new trees grow where the old ones were taken out. It's just a continuous cycle and I've finally realized I'm just part of it all."

Lassiter wasn't sure how he should take all this philosophy all of a sudden. Molly had come to terms with herself about something and if she wanted to tell him what it was, he would be glad to listen. But he still wasn't sure how he fit into it all.

"I have you to thank for waking me up," she went on. "You just showed me the other night that I can still feel good when I'm with someone I want to feel good with. You see, I've spent a long time hating myself and men in general."

"I guess that's why I thought I caused your problems," Lassiter said honestly. "But how did I bring it on?"

"You're a man a woman could care about," Molly said, almost blushing. "I didn't think I had that in me."

"If you've been having such a hard time for so long," Lassiter asked, "then why the good-natured image at the beginning?"

"You see, that was all just a front," Molly confessed. "I spoke to you more than once about being able to shoot that big pistol I have. I had to shoot a man once who kept coming back to rape me. I hated all men for a long time after that, because it seemed to me that all of them wanted to rape me. Now I've realized it isn't fair, that the world goes on and the past should remain in the past."

"It couldn't have been just me that brought you to the realization," Lassiter said.

"Not totally," Molly explained. "But just knowing you have the dimension you do has made me realize I haven't been fair with the men who are good in this world. They're not all out to rape me."

Molly smiled and rode past Lassiter to join Whiskey in preparing the evening meal. She was back to her old self and she considered Lassiter to be the one who had changed her life.

Camp that night was joyous. Dodge City seemed to be just a breeze away now. The hands laughed and told jokes and stories around the fire, and made themselves content to think that the drive would be over soon.

But Lassiter wasn't as eager to call the rest of the drive easy. Nor was Morris. They talked about it in camp that night and both agreed that just because Watt hadn't been seen since Dallas, didn't mean he wasn't still around somewhere. A man like him didn't give up so easily.

It was just before dark when one of the hands on night watch rode into camp to announce that three riders were coming toward the herd. Though Molly didn't want Morris on a horse if there was trouble, he insisted on accompanying Lassiter out of camp to see who the riders were.

All hands remained on alert, ready to climb into the saddle and fight for the herd. But there didn't seem to be any alarm, as Lassiter and Morris returned to camp with the men and had Whiskey fix them something to eat.

"They just jumped us and we didn't have a chance," one of the men was saying. "Them Comanches are treacherous."

The three had been explaining to the hands who had brought them in that they had been attacked by Indians. All the cowhands were gathered around now, listening intently.

The three men had said they were the last of a division of Texas Rangers that had been attacked just a short ways north by Comanches. Morris studied the papers they handed him, and he let Lassiter see them. They looked official enough.

The three were telling about how their captain, a man named Chapman, had been killed—along with the others—and how they were now going to ride around them, to the west, and wanted no more part of the Indians.

The tallest of the three, who was also noticeably the youngest, seemed to Lassiter to be quite nervous. He eyed all the men in camp while a medium, dark-complected man talked about how the three of them had managed to elude the Indians by getting a head-start on their horses.

"It's a good thing they couldn't catch us," the dark-complected one was saying. "Or by now we'd be food for the wolves like the others."

"Weren't you with the other rangers when the Comanches found you?" Lassiter asked him.

It was the shortest one who answered. "We—the three of us here—had just come in from gettin' wood for the fire. We saw the Injuns comin' and just high-tailed it out."

"You didn't stay and fight with your unit?" Lassiter asked.

"There was way too many of them," the dark-complected one insisted. "That would have been suicide."

"You rode out before the Comanches got to your camp?" Lassiter wondered. "Then how do you know for sure that Chapman and the rest of them were killed?"

"Nobody could have survived that many Injuns," the shortest one quickly answered. "I can't see how." He had his head bowed.

"How did you manage to be up there?" Lassiter asked them.

Again the shortest one answered. "We were after a bunch of rustlers that shot up a saloon in Dallas. We got into a shoot-out with them outside of town, then trailed them clean up here. I told Chapman we should've turned back."

The cowhands had already begun to talk among themselves in anxious tones. The last thing they wanted to do was face a war party of angry Comanches.

"What do you think brought the Comanches over here from the Panhandle?" Lassiter asked the men.

"Buffalo hunters," the dark-complected one answered. "Word is, they've been after all the buffalo hunters."

Whiskey and Molly came over with a plate of beans and beef for each of them. The three men eyed Molly—especially the dark-complected one—and began devouring the food.

Lassiter studied them while they ate and listened while Morris asked them questions regarding the gunman named Watt and the gang of rustlers they had been chasing.

The three men discussed how they had caught up with Watt and the others the first night but had lost their trail after that.

"They're hard to keep up with," the short one said through a mouthful of beans. "They ride day and night."

Morris then asked them where they thought Watt and the others had gone. The three men again took turns, relating that after the first night they had never been able to catch up with the gang and figured they were well north by now, possibly as far as Abilene or Dodge City.

"But them Injuns are the worst problem," the short one commented. He spoke directly to Morris now. "If

I was you, I'd move the herd west of here and stay away from them Comanches. That's what I'd do."

Once again the cowhands began to talk among themselves. Most of them agreed with the three men who had come into camp and wanted Morris to turn the herd west to avoid a confrontation with the Comanches. But Lassiter had a few questions he needed answered.

"How long have you been riding since you got rousted by the Comanches?" he asked the short one.

"A couple of days."

"And the Comanches didn't try to track you down?"

". . . Well, no. We rode fast, and they just didn't come after us."

Lassiter nodded. "How far north did this happen?"

"Just south of the Canadian River," the short one answered. He was starting to get nervous and moved from foot to foot and gulped his coffee. "Why you askin' all these questions? We already told you what we know."

"I just want to be sure of what we're up against," Lassiter said. "If we turn the herd, it could mean we lose as much as a week's time in getting to Dodge. We can't afford that."

"It's that or lose everyone to Comanches," the tall one said quickly. "It's your choice."

"Sometimes Indians will barter for a few head of cattle," Lassiter told them. "If they see we have a lot of men and that they could lose some of their warriors, they might be happy to just let us pass and take a few head with them to eat."

Lassiter knew that most Indians preferred buffalo to beef any day. There was a very small chance the Comanches would care at all about the herd. They would eat buffalo as long as the beasts roamed the plains. But he wanted to see how much these men knew and if they were, indeed, Texas Rangers, as they claimed to be.

"I don't know why we should worry about those Comanches," Lassiter said.

The dark-complected one had been eyeing Molly a lot. But he had been listening to what was being said and he turned to Lassiter.

"Maybe you don't know Injuns," he said. "They'll take your *remuda* quicker than you can blink."

Lassiter nodded. He could see that at least one of them had been working on the trail for his living—whether or not he earned it as a Texas Ranger.

"We've got enough men to watch our horses," Lassiter said.

"You think what you want," the dark-complected one told Lassiter. "But you know as well as I do that them Comanches are unpredictable. You just don't know how they'll think. So, maybe you don't care if the herd gets through or not. But come mornin' we're headin' west and out of here."

The three men went off by themselves and spread their bedrolls on the edge of camp. The hands all gathered and all they talked about was Colmanches and what they did to white men—and women. They wanted no part of a fight with them.

Lassiter spoke with Morris and learned that Morris also wanted to take the three men's advice about moving the herd west.

"Why haven't we seen signs if there are Indians in the area?" Lassiter asked. "I've worked as a scout a number of times and I haven't seen a thing to indicate we're in any trouble. I just don't know about those three."

"Maybe they rode in from the north," Morris suggested. "There's nothing to say they'd take the same trails as we do."

"Maybe you're right," Lassiter acknowledged. "But we'll lose a lot of time."

"We can't afford to be attacked by Comanches," Morris was saying. "We'd lose some if not all the herd, and likely a lot of men. I'd rather lose time than cattle and men."

Lassiter was thinking. He kept looking over to the edge of camp, where the three men were bedding down, and he kept wondering.

"I just have a feeling about those three," Lassiter told Morris. "I just don't know about them."

"You saw their papers," Morris said. "Don't you think they're rangers?"

"I don't know," Lassiter said. "But come morning, I want to talk to them some more. I want to know for sure."

16

IT WAS LATE BEFORE the camp settled down. The hands on watch were nervous and those in their bedrolls had trouble getting themselves to relax.

Lassiter couldn't sleep either. But it wasn't because he was worried about Comanches. He tossed and turned in his bedroll and grew more and more concerned about the three men who had come into camp saying they were Texas Rangers. He had no means of disproving them, but he was almost certain they were imposters.

He thought more about the three and finally got up and began pacing around, looking toward the edge of camp where the three men were sleeping. Their horses were saddled and picketed close to them, as were all the hands' horses. If suddenly something should happen, they would be ready to mount up and ride immediately.

Lassiter stood thinking in the darkness. The crickets were loud and shrill. From the distance came the sounds of wolves yapping and howling to the nearly full moon that shone down from the open sky. There were getting to be a lot of wolves these days, as the buffalo hunters were leaving a lot of spoils for them.

Lassiter heard a sound behind him and turned to see Molly coming down from the back of the wagon. She walked over to him, a shawl wrapped around her shoulders, and asked what was bothering him.

"I have a bad feeling about those three men who claim to be Texas Rangers," Lassiter told her under his breath. "I want to check them out real close."

"Who do you think they are if they're not rangers?" she asked.

"I don't know. Maybe rustlers. I'm just not sure."

"Some of Watt's men?"

"Could be."

"How would they get the identification papers of Texas Rangers?" Molly asked.

"I don't know," Lassiter answered. "And I can't figure what good it would do them to try and make us think they're rangers."

"Didn't they say they thought we should move the herd farther west?" Molly said after some thought. "Maybe there's a plan to take the herd, and it would be easier for them if the herd was going up the trail west of here."

Lassiter nodded. "Could be. That just might be the reason."

Suddenly, there was a yell from one of the cowhands on night duty that there were riders approaching. Lassiter and Morris both called for all hands to get up and be ready to ride. Immediately the camp was a flurry of men scurrying to find their guns and their horses.

The hands were all ready for trouble, and Lassiter and Morris had to caution them against shooting blindly without knowing what or who they were firing at. They would know soon enough who the riders were.

Then one of the hands on night watch rode into camp and announced that there were more Texas Rangers coming in. The riders who were coming in were also saying that they were rangers.

Lassiter looked over to where the three men had rolled out of their beds. They didn't seem alarmed. But Lassiter still wondered.

Two more of the hands on night watch brought the riders into camp. There were four of them, worn and tired and bloody. Three of them had sustained minor flesh wounds in a fight of some kind, and they soon disclosed that they were the true survivors of the fight with Watt and the rustlers.

"They about got us all," a man named Hanson said, dismounting and holding his arm tightly to his side. It was swollen and discolored just below the shoulder.

He said he was now in charge of what was left of the unit. He told of the fight with the rustlers and how Watt had started a decoy fire to set them up. It had worked. Now Chapman and the rest were dead, and they intended to track Watt and the others until they found them.

"What about the Comanches?" Lassiter asked them.

Hanson looked at Lassiter. "What Comanches?"

Lassiter and Morris both looked around for the three men who had been sleeping at the edge of camp. There was a scream and the dark-complected one stepped into the light of the fire. He had a gun to Molly's head.

"Let go of me!" Molly yelled. She fought and kicked and finally broke free of him. But he quickly grabbed her again and cocked the pistol in her face.

"I ain't got nothin' to lose," he told Molly. He

looked to everyone in camp. "I mean it. If you figure to take me, she goes first."

Molly held herself tense. She wanted to pull away again, but his eyes were wild.

"Molly, don't move," Lassiter advised. "He'll kill you. He's that crazy."

"She's leavin' with us," the rustler said, pulling Molly backwards.

"No!" she yelled.

"Just hold on," Lassiter told her. "You won't be with them long."

The dark-complected rustler held Molly tighter to him and laughed. "Just long enough, though."

Lassiter and Morris and the others started forward toward the rustler. He fired his gun in the air, just over Molly's head.

"I mean it!" he yelled. "Next one takes her head off."

Everyone backed away and the dark-complected rustler pulled Molly farther back against him and put the barrel of his revolver in her ear.

"We're goin' to leave, real peaceful like," he said, backing away, while the other two rustlers came forward with their horses. "If anybody follows us, the little lady dies. Just remember that." He was looking directly at Lassiter.

Lassiter and Morris and the others stood helpless while the dark-haired rustler put Molly on his horse and climbed up behind her. He held the reins tight in one hand and put the barrel of his pistol in her ribs.

"Just remember, nobody comes after us," he warned again, kicking his horse into a run.

They were quickly lost in the darkness and the men all began to grumble angrily. Whiskey was in favor of going after them right away, but Lassiter told him that the three were too trigger happy.

"But there's no tellin' what they'll do to her," Whiskey said.

"They haven't got time to stop for that," Lassiter said. "They need to reach Watt and tell him their plan failed. Once they get to him, then we have to worry. But I'll catch them before that."

"We'll go with you," Hanson said. "We've come this far after them. It's no time to quit now."

Hanson looked to the others and they all nodded and talked among themselves. They wanted to avenge Chapman's death in the worst way. And they were curious as to how the three rustlers got into camp in the first place.

Lassiter explained that the three had showed up with papers to show they were Texas Rangers. Somehow they had come by documents that had belonged to Texas Rangers, but who were now likely dead.

Hanson nodded. He then related that the four of them had finally gone back to bury Chapman and the others and had found three of them stripped naked.

"At first we thought they wanted it to look like the Comanches had done it," Hanson said. "But the men weren't butchered like Comanches would have done. So we couldn't figure it out. It appears they had some trap set for you as well."

"They've been after this herd since we started," Morris said. "I don't expect them to give up now."

It was decided that Lassiter and the four rangers would go after the three rustlers and Molly. Morris would move the herd up the trail as usual and they would meet as soon as they had taken Molly back—if that was possible.

That wouldn't be easy, and it wouldn't be good to rush it. As hard as it was to keep his composure, Lassiter sat with Morris and the four rangers and had coffee for nearly an hour. They planned their advance against the three rustlers, detailing how they would split into two groups when they knew for sure they were closing in on them.

Lassiter was worried that the three would reach Watt and the rest of the rustlers before they could catch up with them. But he knew it would be putting Molly's life in certain danger if they decided to just ride pell-mell after them. The rustler had been right— he had nothing to lose by killing Molly.

Lassiter mounted his black stallion and left camp with the four rangers. He took a deep breath as he led them out into the darkness. Dawn would be breaking before long and he could only hope that they reached the rustlers before it was too late for Molly.

Molly sat on the horse in front of the dark-complected rustler, more angry than afraid. She had been around death and dying so often that she now took fate for granted.

And she had resolved she had finally gotten over the rape ordeal she had been through a few years before. Now she was certainly not going to allow these men to take any liberties with her, not unless they had killed her first.

They had been riding for what seemed like hours. The night had brought many sights and sounds—and smells. Even the darkness couldn't hide the stench of rotting buffalo corpses they had passed not far back. Molly was just glad the night could hide the scene from her.

It wasn't long before dawn was breaking in the eastern sky. According to what she was hearing from the three rustlers, they should be reaching the main camp with Watt and the others before much longer. They were apparently located along a small stream to the north and west.

She knew that Lassiter wasn't far behind now, as he would certainly be coming for her. She felt confident he would catch up to them, for they had had to travel slow due to the extra weight on the horse she was riding with the dark-complected rustler. She knew that she had to make them slow now even more, or they would reach Watt and the others, and Lassiter wouldn't have a chance to get her free from them.

She listened as the three of them talked about getting back to Watt. Bauer, the short one, worried that Watt would be angry about the plan's failure. But the dark-complected one, Markley, was confident that he would be glad to see they had captured the woman. He knew from the look on Lassiter's face that the woman was special to him.

"Maybe we can get Lassiter by himself," Markley suggested. "Have him come and get this little lady." He poked Molly in the ribs with the barrel of his pistol. "Then we can get rid of him and make it easy to take the herd."

"Sure as hell he'll be on our trail," Bauer pointed out. "I say we set up an ambush."

Skip, the youngest and tallest, had said very little up until now. He was just glad to be out of the camp and had worried all along that something would go wrong.

"We were just lucky the woman was close to us, so we could get her," he told the others.

Markley was laughing. He leaned ahead and whispered into Molly's ear.

"You're goin' to get a taste of a real man now. Real soon."

Molly tried to hold back her anger. She began to think, realizing that she might now have a chance to detain these men—maybe long enough to allow Lassiter to catch up. But she didn't want to think what might happen if she allowed them to stop with her and Lassiter didn't make it in time.

They rode on farther and Markley began to put his hands all over her. She fought to keep from yelling and when she couldn't stand it any more, she swung her leg over and jumped down from the horse.

Markley cocked his pistol. "Where do you think you're goin'?"

"Shoot me," Molly said. "You'll have to before I let you put your hands on me again."

"We'll see about that," Markley said, getting down from his horse.

"Wait!" Bauer called out to Markley. "Hold on just a minute."

"What's the matter with you?"

Bauer was looking far out toward the north. He mentioned that he was sure he could see riders out there, a number of them, riding toward them. They were still a long distance away, but they would be coming closer. And he was certain they were Indians.

"I doubt it," Markley said. He was still considering going after Molly.

"They sure as hell ain't buffalo," Bauer insisted, still looking out into the early light. "We'd best take some cover and stay quiet."

"Bauer's right," Skip put in. He had stayed quiet, but now he was really frightened. "We've got to hide. And get our horses down in the grass."

"You two are just fidgety is all," Markley said.

"Just look and tell me what you see out there," Bauer said, pointing toward the north.

Now Skip spoke up. He was pointing toward the south. "Five riders," he said. "Lassiter's got to be one of them. He's got to be."

Now the riders from the north were coming closer and the riders from the south were moving in as well.

Markley finally consented to Skip and Bauer's wishes that they sit tight behind a nearby small hill just off the trail and wait to see what would happen. Markley tied Molly up and finally decided that their situation was serious.

"We'll just wait here, real quiet," he said to the other two. "There ain't no place else to go, I guess."

Skip's eyes were big and Bauer was cursing under his breath. "There ain't nothin' to do but just wait," Bauer said. "We ain't got a choice."

17

DAWN NOW FILLED THE SKY with a glow that spread quickly across the plains. A breeze was blowing, promising to make the day hot. All across the distance, the gusts of wind whipped through the tall grass, making it a sea of waving green.

Lassiter led the four rangers onward, following the trail of the three rustlers with Molly. The grass was parted where they had ridden and it was easy to see they were headed north and west.

Lassiter was certain they had made good time and had almost caught up with the rustlers. The next step was to determine right where the three were headed with Molly and try to cut them off.

The rangers told Lassiter about a camping site commonly used along a tributary of the South Canadian River. The tracks were leading right in that direction. Lassiter remembered what the saloon girl in the Steer's Head had told him about a plan Watt had put together to get the herd at the South Canadian. Maybe it was designed in conjunction with turning the herd into hostile Indian territory.

After some discussion, Lassiter and the rangers concluded that Watt and the others were likely waiting at the campsite. That site wasn't more than seven or eight miles ahead and Lassiter knew they had to move quickly, for the rustlers couldn't be more than a couple of miles ahead of them now.

It was decided that they would split into the two groups, swing around from two sides and hopefully converge on the rustlers before they got to the river. That was the only chance they had.

Three rangers left and one stayed with Lassiter. He hurried his black stallion and the ranger followed. They spoke little, knowing what had to be done.

Farther on the stench of raw buffalo carcasses came to Lassiter as thick as rotten smoke. Lassiter curled his lip as he topped a rise and then rode across a flat littered with the skinned corpses of nearly a hundred buffalo.

"That's not a pretty sight," the ranger said. "I can see the reason the Comanches are warring."

Lassiter and the ranger crossed the flat and watched while packs of wolves snarled over the rotting remains. But Lassiter had other things to think about and he pushed on in hopes of getting in front of the three rustlers soon.

In the extreme distance, Lassiter could see a thin line of green that was formed by isolated trees along the small stream. He knew that he and the ranger would have to hurry now, for every moment counted in the chase after the rustlers.

The rustlers' trail went through the grass past a low hill, just off to the left, and in the early light of the morning Lassiter detected a glint of sunlight off metal.

"Get down!" Lassiter yelled to the ranger riding beside him. "Ambush!"

Lassiter ducked as the rifles opened up on them. Lassiter heard bullets whizzing by him as he jumped from the saddle and laid his stallion down in the cover of the tall grass.

But the ranger was not so lucky, He yelled and clutched at his chest as he tumbled from the saddle and sprawled in the grass next to Lassiter. His horse jumped forward and ran off.

Knowing he needed more than his twin Colt pistols for protection, Lassiter took his Winchester .44 rifle from its scabbard and moved away from his stallion through the tall grass. He moved slowly, careful not to move any more stalks of grass than he could help. The wind itself was moving the grass, but a man in a hurry could be easily spotted.

Lassiter took position a good ways from his stallion. He watched through the grass while his horse stood up and wandered away. Then he ducked down again when he heard voices that gradually worked their way toward where his horse had been.

That was good. They thought he had fallen where the stallion had been. And they were going right to the spot.

As he expected, they were the three rustlers. And from the sounds of their discussion, it appeared as if they thought they had killed him.

Markley was laughing while he spoke.

"I figure I gut-shot him by the way he doubled over. Think so, Bauer? Don't you think so?" He began to laugh again in a manic, wheezing tone.

Bauer only grunted. "We'd better find him and get his head for Watt. If them Comanches are near here, they'll come down on us after hearin' the shots."

Lassiter stayed low in the grass while the three

advanced closer. He wondered what they had done with Molly and if she had been harmed. He would have to worry about that later, as the three were nearly to where he had gone down into the grass. In but a few moments they would realize he wasn't dead.

He did not want to take the chance on being spotted and he would have to rise from his position to even begin to see through the tall grass. There was a chance he could drop all three if he got off three good shots, but it was too risky. He would have to let them discover he was not dead, then go at them one by one.

"He's not here!" Markley growled, looking carefully through the flattened grass where Lassiter and the horse had lowered themselves. "I know I hit him."

"I don't see no blood," Bauer commented. "Spread out. We have to get him now."

"I'm goin' back and get the girl," Markley announced. "That way we've got the odds with us."

Lassiter could wait no longer and rose from the grass. The three men were twenty feet from him and he could see their startled faces a split second before he fired a shot into Markley's chest. He dropped with a scream.

Bauer and Skip both reacted quickly and brought their guns up to fire. In a flash of movement, Lassiter dropped back down again into the grass and jumped sideways from his position just as a stream of bullets clipped the grass like angry bees, right where he had been crouched.

Then suddenly the firing stopped.

Lassiter heard the men running through the grass back toward the hill. He rose to see them go around the hill and then watched while they rode out, kicking their horses into a dead run. In but a few moments, both Bauer and Skip were topping a rise to the north on their horses, riding like two wild men.

They were gone before Lassiter could aim and fire. And he could see the reason for their sudden reaction wasn't him. Not far away was a number of mounted Comanches.

A large part of the warriors separated off and kicked their ponies into a dead run after the two rustlers. They rode low over the ponies' backs, like they were part of the animals. Lassiter knew the two didn't stand a chance.

Lassiter considered hurrying over to where the rustlers had set up their ambush. He wanted to look for Molly. But the Comanches were watching him closely.

Lassiter began to work himself into a fighting mood, a mood that could mean life or death in just a short time.

He hurried over to where his black stallion stood grazing. The other warriors began riding toward him, waiting for him to mount and start his own horse into a run.

But Lassiter had no intention of doing that. He knew that to show fear would mean certain death. He still wanted to locate Molly, but he realized he would have to wait until after the encounter with the Comanches. If they knew she was there, it would certainly make it harder for him to fight them.

Lassiter pulled a canteen from his saddle and drank calmly. He intended to show the oncoming warriors that he had no fear of them. He calculated his odds, based on what he saw them doing as they approached. They seemed to be in no particular hurry.

Lassiter put his canteen back and began to slap his hands against his black leather vest. He took off his gunbelt and ejected the bullets from his rifle, so that the warriors could see he would fight hand-to-hand.

The oncoming warriors already realized he would not run from them, and that since he was showing signs of anger rather than fear, he must be a respectable fighter. The Comanche, like most warring tribes, preferred to take their glory in singular achievement. It was likely they would try to size him up and allow one of their number to try and kill him in hand-to-hand combat.

Lassiter continued to worry about Molly. He was not even sure she had been with the rustlers now. He could not hear anything coming from the grass behind the hill. He worried they had possibly abused her back along the trail and had left her for dead.

Then, from where the rustlers had hurried to get away, there came a series of high-pitched screams. There was no doubt the other warriors had gotten to the fleeing rustlers. It was hard to tell what they were doing to them, but knives often brought those kinds of screams from people.

Then in but a few minutes, Lassiter could see the first group of warriors rejoining the second. The two rustlers were with them, and from what Lassiter could see in the distance they appeared to be more dead than alive.

Lassiter casually climbed onto his stallion. He held the empty rifle in the crook of his arm and waited. The Comanches came toward him at a gallop now and soon were no longer images in the distance, but a formation of death, like painted shadows on horseback.

There were nineteen warriors who topped the hill and spread out in a line. The two rustlers were being dragged behind two horses, their arms held by rawhide ropes. A number of arrows protruded from them, some driven clear through. Both men were still conscious and moaning when the warriors dragged them up for Lassiter to see.

Lassiter showed them he could make sign.

"They are no brothers of mine," he told them, using

his hands. "Do what you want with them. Then I will deal with you, when you are finished."

They studied Lassiter from ponies that danced with the urge to run, for which they were bred. The warriors were a mass of paint, of red and black and yellow, and even white when the warrior's medicine demanded the color. They wore the wings and talons of various birds of prey in their hair or suspended from their necks and arms. Wolf tails were hanging from their lances and medicine shields and bear claws could be seen around the necks of a few warriors.

In the middle of the column of warriors was the most honored among them. He was also sitting a black horse and Lassiter saw numerous tassles hanging from his bright red breechclout down the side of his horse. He was heavily painted in yellow and black and his long hair was braided with otter fur. Hanging from his scalplock was a single eagle feather.

Lassiter knew who this warrior was instantly. He had heard of this feared Comanche, honored more than any other among his people. It was Quanah Parker.

Those who knew of Quanah Parker realized his influence among the Kwahadi band of Comanche. The son of a prominent warrior and a white woman captive, Quanah Parker had risen to prominence among the Comanche and was now their main leader. Now he was out for blood across their revered hunting grounds.

Lassiter continued to sit his horse calmly, awaiting the first move by the warriors. He knew the warriors viewed this as honorable—but they would still want to kill him.

They suddenly began tactics to try and disturb Lassiter. A group of warriors dismounted and set to work on Skip and Bauer with their knives. Their screams rose into the air and subsided only when the knives finally ended their lives.

Lassiter could tell the warriors were waiting for him to turn his horse and run, to show them he was a coward. But he still sat his horse calmly.

This time he made sign language directly to Quanah Parker. He informed Quanah Parker he had wanted to do the same thing to the two men but that the Kwahadi had beat him to it. He ended by telling Quanah Parker that they should go back to their people and not disturb him, for he could easily send any one of them to the next life, if that was what they wished.

Quanah Parker did not answer Lassiter back, but it was obvious he and all his warriors were startled by the bold affront to their power. They watched while Lassiter pointed to the dead rustlers at their feet.

"You treat your enemies with more tenderness than I ever would," Lassiter continued in sign. "Could it be that you are only children?"

Lassiter watched as some of the warriors covered their mouths with their hands, the sign of immense surprise. This was the last thing they had expected.

"I am a spirit dressed in black," Lassiter told them. "I have come to find you, and this is a good day to die!"

Lassiter felt this was the time to impress them even further. He stripped off his shirt and threw it to the ground. He pointed to various locations on his chest and stomach where he had received various wounds over the years. Then he took from his saddlebag a small knife and cut a gash across his left forearm. The blood ran in a smooth flow.

Quickly, Lassiter then dipped the first and index fingers of his right hand into his own blood and slowly began tracing circles around his old wounds, marks of honor on a fighting warrior's body. Many of the Kwahhadi Comanche on the hill who now watched him had the same kind of circles around their own wounds, made from vermilion or red clay paint. But Lassiter's move in using his own blood impressed them.

He painted himself slowly and deliberately, knowing he needed every advantage possible. This told the warriors he had survived many fights and couldn't be killed. He was a ghost, he said, and was destined to wear black and bring terrible death to those who wished to harm him.

The warriors talked more among themselves. Some of them were unsure they wanted to stay. But others didn't believe Lassiter and wanted to see him die.

Finally, one rider came forward. Lassiter was being honored by facing a strong and proud warrior in battle. Normally white men held little honor for the warriors who killed them and often they were not given even the dignity of a scalping, for their hair—the outward symbol of their strength—was considered no trophy.

But these Kwahadi Comanche, including Quanah Parker himself, now knew they were facing an exceptional enemy.

The warrior who had come forward now pulled a knife from his side and placed it between his teeth. He motioned to his fellow warriors that his medicine was strong and that the white man with the strong character was no ghost and would not see the sun fall behind the horizon this day. He wanted to prove that Lassiter was afraid of him—not like a ghost, which fears nothing.

The warrior then kicked his pony into a dead run down the hill at Lassiter. He raised his lance and screamed through the blade between his teeth, his war shield in front of him. Lassiter did not move, but sat his fidgety black stallion and waited.

The warrior came in a burst of speed and power and

the others marveled at Lassiter's courage. When the warrior turned his pony and raced across the bottom of the hill in front of him, Lassiter still did not react.

The warrior raced past Lassiter again, looking back, unable to believe he hadn't scared this strange warrior dressed in black. Perhaps he was a ghost after all. He didn't think so, and would soon find out for himself.

18

LASSITER WATCHED THE WARRIORS stare at him from the back of his own horse. Lassiter nodded to himself; he knew he had dented the warrior's confidence and by so doing, had brought concern to the other warriors. Now even if they all came at him at once, he would kill some of them, and that would bring dishonor to those who died. They would not go into the next life as proud warriors.

But the warrior who had ridden down at Lassiter was not to be denied. He would try another tactic: there was something he would show Lassiter before they fought.

At the bottom of the hill the warrior turned his horse at a right angle to Lassiter, with merely the touch of a knee. The pony lurched into full speed and ran headlong through the grass with a burst of power.

In an instant the warrior was standing on the horse's back with his lance raised high in the air, yelling oaths at Lassiter. Quickly, he was back down upon the pony's back and turned to ride in a tight circle around

Lassiter, jamming the lance into the ground during the quick turn. Now he began his demonstration of horsemanship.

Lassiter watched while the warrior kicked the horse into full speed, then let himself down alongside the horse's right flank and then pulled himself under the stomach and up the other side. Without stopping his movement, the warrior continued up and over the head and under the neck until he had placed himself in a sitting position back atop the horse.

He had now completed the circle around Lassiter and pulled his lance from the ground. He sat his horse to see if Lassiter was intimidated by the show.

With his eyes up the hill on Quanah Parker, Lassiter made sign that this warrior has ridden well but that he would hear his death song if he still intended to fight.

The warrior had gone too far to stop now, and he turned his pony and made sign that he intended to kill the white warrior dressed in black.

"You had better tell him his glory will not come," Lassiter made sign to Quanah Parker. "For this is my day and anyone who falls to me will cry out as a ghost forever."

Again the warriors talked among themselves, many of them with their hands over their mouths again.

Lassiter now made sign to Quanah Parker that he would go in peace if they would do the same. Quanah Parker looked from warrior to warrior and let them decide. Most of them wanted to leave Lassiter alone— he was likely what he said, a black ghost.

But the warrior who had first challenged Lassiter had no intention of leaving. He told Lassiter in sign that he didn't think he was a ghost at all. He knew he was a strong warrior, but no ghost. He would prove it by killing him and eating his heart.

Quanah Parker, for the first time, spoke to Lassiter

in sign. He told Lassiter he didn't think he was a ghost either, but that it was too bad he had white skin—for he showed he had a brave heart.

"We shall see how truely great a white warrior you are," Quanah Parker told him in sign.

Lassiter was sure now that he was going to have to fight the warrior that sat his horse a short ways from him. But he would try to keep from fighting one more time.

He told Quanah Parker again that it was not a good day for any of the Kwahadi Comanche to die. If the warrior came at him, he would die, and he would not get a chance to live normally in the afterlife.

"Hear me well," Lassiter told Quanah Parker and the others in sign. "I wear black and am known as a dark warrior. He who dies at my hands will be destined to roam this world as a ghost. I have told you that before. This is the last time I will speak."

By then the warriors were no longer stunned at anything Lassiter said. He had power. To the warriors who wished to leave, it stunned them more, though, to hear him speak of his powers and his black leathers. It made them wonder if they should stay. A few of them decided not to and quickly rode away, so they might not be cast under a spell by this warrior dressed in black.

But the warrior facing Lassiter had made up his mind. The challenge had been made. The warrior now pulled his lance from the ground and kicked his horse into a full run toward Lassiter.

At the mere touch of the spurs, Lassiter's stallion surged into full speed and he rode to meet the charging warrior head-on. As the warrior's lance came toward him Lassiter smashed it with the butt of the rifle, shattering it and sending the Kwahadi warrior off his horse with the blow.

The knife flew from the warrior's mouth into the grass and Lassiter jumped down from his stallion to get it. The warrior struggled to his feet and found Lassiter coming at him with his own knife. Quanah Parker watched and listened while his warriors talked among themselves about this strange and powerful white warrior. What he had said was going to come true.

Stunned and shocked at Lassiter's own horsemanship, and his quickness, the warrior fumbled at his belt to draw another knife. But it was too late. Lassiter attacked and though the warrior tried to dodge the thrust, the blade went across his chest, slicing away the bottom half of his lungs.

This caused the warrior to double over. But Lassiter grabbed him by the hair and had him fall backward and bounce in the grass, gasping for air. Lassiter then stood on the warrior's legs as the blood came out of the low chest wound as froth.

Lassiter then turned to the other warriors, who were now watching with their hands over their mouths.

"I told you he would remain as a ghost," Lassiter told them. "See how his spirit screams for release, but cannot escape."

The warrior was dying rapidly. But in his last throes of life, his lungs tried desperately to bring air into his body. In so doing, they enhanced the bleeding process and made it appear as if the warrior's chest had a life of its own.

Lassiter raised the blade into the air for Quanah Parker and the other warriors to see. They had lost one of their number, as he had promised, and they feared that the warrior's spirit would certainly remain there, as Lassiter had promised.

"If any one of you come down here to kill me,"

Lassiter said in sign language. "This warrior's spirit will be with you always, so that you might free him."

None of the warriors, including Quanah Parker, wanted anything more to do with Lassiter. They were now convinced that his black clothes were a symbol that he was indeed a spirit, a bad spirit, and that he could not really be killed.

"It would be good if you left this area entirely," Lassiter told the warriors. "I will be with a group of the slow buffalo, and they will be going through the lands—not to stay, but just to pass through."

Lassiter got back on his black stallion and waited. He watched the warriors take their fallen brother's body and leave immediately. They were singing songs to the sky, which Lassiter knew to be to their spirit helpers. They wanted protection from Lassiter's strange powers.

When they were gone, Lassiter turned for the other side of the hill and found Molly lying on her side, her mouth gagged and her hands and feet tied. She was delighted to see Lassiter.

"I thought surely you were dead," she told him. "Did you come alone?"

"No," Lassiter answered. "The four rangers came with me. Three of them broke off and we were supposed to meet up ahead. The one that came with me was killed. We'll take him back to the herd and bury him. I just hope the others aren't dead as well."

Lassiter told Molly how he and the rangers had come after the three rustlers, hoping to jump them and surprise them—then get her away from them.

He talked while he helped her rub the blood back into her hands and feet. He told her what had happened with the Comanches as well. She was relieved to know that they were likely going to leave the area.

Then she went to his arms and he held her for a

time. She was exhausted from the ordeal, but knew she couldn't rest until they got back to the herd.

Lassiter put her on the back of his horse and climbed on. He looked in the distance more than once to try and see the three rangers who had split off from him. But they were nowhere in sight. He could only hope that they were someplace where they didn't run into Watt's men unexpectedly.

And there were still the Comanche warriors to consider. Even though he had scared them, Lassiter knew they wouldn't remain cautious for long. They would be looking for more buffalo hunters soon, and anyone else they might find. He just hoped they didn't take the information he had given them about the herd as a challenge.

Watt walked toward the top of a low hill just out from the river. He fingered the notch in his ear while he walked, thinking that the bullet wound from Lassiter's gun was healing, but that he was still going to kill the man—no matter what it took.

He wondered about the three who had gone into the Bar 9 camp and professed to be rangers. The plan should be taking shape by now, Watt concluded, and the herd should be on its way toward where they were waiting.

Three of the rustlers were at the top of the hill already, motioning for him to hurry and climb up with them. He yelled up for them to relax, but one of them commented he was watching three riders coming toward them.

Watt wondered if it might be the three who had gone into camp. But why would they be back so soon? Hadn't the plan worked.

Watt immediately became concerned. He hurried now and fought for breath at the top of the hill. He could see three riders still at least three to four miles away, coming in their direction.

"You figure that's Markley and Bauer and Skip?" one of the rustlers asked Watt.

"It's likely," Watt answered. "I don't know of any other three who'd know this place."

Some of the other rustlers on the hill began to point and talk excitedly. They were looking not far behind the first three riders, across the plains to where a large group of riders were coming up on the first three.

"Those are Comanches, or I'll miss my guess," one of the rustlers stated emphatically. "And those three are sittin' ducks."

"So are we," another rustler stated.

"Time to get out of here," Watt said without hesitation.

"What about Markley and Bauer and Skip?" one of the rustlers asked Watt. "They'll die out there."

Watt was starting down the hill. He turned to the rustler. "You go ahead out there and help them. I'm going to get moving or them Comanches will be here after they finish with them. I ain't ready for no fight with them."

One of the rustlers now pointed out to where the Indians had kicked their ponies into a dead run. Watt came back up where he could see clearly and remarked that it was certainly time to leave.

They all watched while the three riders disappeared into a small draw a good distance out. The warriors then split up into groups and fanned out around the draw, going down into it from different directions. Whoever the three men were didn't stand a chance.

"Let's go," Watt insisted. "They'll be tied up butchering whoever that is for some time—just long enough for us to get away."

Watt and the others hurried to their horses and

crossed the river. Once on the other side, they set to riding due north. All of them were nearly certain the three men had been their comrades and there was a long period of silence while they rode across the seemingly endless expanse of grass.

"Skip wasn't old enough to die," one of them remarked sullenly.

"None of them were old enough," one other added.

Nothing more was said for a long distance, until someone asked Watt if they were now going to implement the plan to take the herd at the crossing up ahead on the South Canadian River.

"We should have stuck to that to begin with," one of the rustlers said with disgust. "This idea of runnin' the herd into the Injuns wasn't all that smart."

Some of the others agreed, while the rest remained silent. There was no argument in the fact that they couldn't afford to lose the additional three men that had seemingly just died at the hands of Comanches.

But the idea of getting the Bar 9 cowhands into the heart of the Comanches had seemed sound. If it had worked, taking the herd would have been a lot easier.

Now they would work their last and soundest plan at the crossing on the South Canadian. They traveled at a steady pace, keeping themselves at least two days ahead of the herd. The crossing would be their last chance to try for the herd and be guaranteed a better than average chance of getting most or all of the longhorns.

It was mid-morning of a hot day when Watt led the rustlers to the banks of the South Canadian. He studied the river and smiled. It was flowing moderately, but was still deep enough to hide the bottom.

He continued to smile as he worked a sign out of the ground that read: QUICKSAND. The herds that had passed through before had erected the sign as a warning to cross farther up the river, that the recent rains had brought in heavy amounts of sand, making the bottom treacherous.

Watt and the rustlers took the sign to the crossing farther upriver and placed it in the ground there. If Lassiter or anyone scouting ahead saw the sign, they would suggest the herd cross at the lower ford now.

"This should slow them up enough for us to get to them," Watt said, feeling proud of himself. "Now all we have to do is wait."

19

LASSITER HAD BEEN AT the South Canadian for over an hour, inspecting the regular crossing. He was disturbed, as there was a sign that warned of quicksand.

He wondered at the sign, as there was good indication that other herds had crossed over at this ford in the recent past. The trail showed use and there didn't seem to be any indication that cattle had bogged down or that men had been lost.

Not far back was another crossing, which seemed to be the worst of all of them. He felt that if the sign should be anywhere, it should be there. But he also knew that the bottom was deceptive and that if there was a herd that had passed through and had encountered trouble, they would certainly have left a sign to warn others behind them.

Lassiter decided to talk it over with Morris and they could make the decision together. The herd was now pushing into view and Lassiter rode back to direct Morris and the others in the lead. The herd was stopped and allowed to graze for a time while Lassiter and Morris discussed the situation.

"I'd say we'd better use this first ford, if there's a sign at the main one warning of quicksand," Morris advised. "We'll just have to take it real slow."

Lassiter told him that the main trail had been the one used the most often, but conceded that a flash flood might have come through and deposited a lot of sediment in its wake.

"We haven't got that far to Dodge now," Morris was saying. "The hands are tired of the drive. Let's just get the herd across."

Lassiter thought a moment. "Why don't we push just fifty head across to begin with?" he finally suggested. "That way we can test the bottom and not have the whole herd going in at once."

Morris accepted the idea as sound and he and Lassiter worked with the other hands to cut fifty head free from the main herd. They quickly began to drive them toward the river.

As the longhorn steers held up at the river's edge, Lassiter urged his black stallion out beside them. The horse seemed to be secure in its footing and Lassiter turned the stallion around and came back out of the water.

"I'm still concerned, though," Lassiter stated frankly. "The footing at the shore is likely far better than farther out in the channel. And if we get those heavy longhorns bogged down out there, they'll drown before we can get a rope on them and pull them out."

There was no alternative but to drive the small bunch into the river and see what happened. They would have to cross somewhere sooner or later and there was no sense in wasting time now.

The longhorns moved into the river with an urge to reach the opposite shore. Lassiter and two other hands rode on one side of the group, while Morris and another hand took the opposite side. The steers seemed content with the crossing until suddenly, one of them bogged down.

It was a steer right next to Morris. At the same time, Morris's horse lost its footing as well and the two animals sank to their haunches before anyone knew what was happening, trapped against one another in the sticky bottom.

Morris yelled, as his leg was caught between his horse and the steer. Both animals were floundering badly and Morris was getting his injured hip worked over badly.

One of the hands on Morris's side tried to ride his horse over to help, but the horse refused to work its way out into the treacherous quicksand. Morris kept yelling and pushing on the bogged steer's back, trying to get his leg lose from between the two animals.

By now other steers were getting bogged down as well, and Lassiter's black stallion began to dance backward to avoid a low spot just ahead, where the river water boiled like hot soup.

A number of the steers began to thrash and bawl, only getting themselves deeper into the heavy sands. The other hands were by now coming out from shore, throwing ropes over the bogged longhorns.

Lassiter could see no way to reach Morris, who was by now nearly passed out from the pain. Lassiter yelled across at him to keep working, to keep trying to get his leg loose. But Morris's horse was as frantic as the longhorn, and they were both going down together.

Lassiter turned his black stallion around and rode back out of the river. He came around and urged the black down into the water again. The stallion was reluctant to make the journey back out into the treacherous current. But at Lassiter's urging, the horse surged into the water once more.

In less than a minute, Lassiter was alongside Morris, throwing a rope over him. By now the steer had drowned and was half-floating, leaning against another steer who was close to death as well.

The steer's death allowed Morris to move his leg. But he couldn't get it out of the stirrup, as his horse had sunk down below the level of Morris's knees, and was now thrashing in a crazed effort to save itself.

The horse still had its head above water when Lassiter grabbed the reins and pulled the animal sideways. The horse, nearly exhausted, still responded and with a great effort, surged upward and brought its front feet out of the mire.

One of the horse's forelegs struck solid footing underneath and with renewed hope, the animal snorted and worked with all its might to free itself. Finally, the horse was out of the mire and Lassiter led it to shore, where it stood shaking uncontrollably.

Morris was still nearly unconscious. His will to live had brought him a great deal of strength and Lassiter had to talk to him for a time and work with him to get his hands pried loose from the saddle horn.

Molly helped Lassiter get him down and spread out upon the ground. He twisted and turned in agony, but there was no way to tell how badly he had reinjured the wound.

The hands were still working to save as many of the steers as they could. Lassiter knew he had to go back into the river and help them, or they would all be lost. But suddenly there was another emergency that need his full response.

"Rustlers!" a hand that was riding hard from the main herd yelled. "All of you, come! Rustlers!"

The herd was already in a stampede as Lassiter

looked out from where Whiskey had brought the wagon up to help with Morris. The dust was thick but Lassiter knew Watt and his men were alongside the longhorns, yelling and shooting their pistols into the air.

Lassiter helped Molly and Whiskey move Morris into the back of the wagon. Whiskey had a rifle ready and Molly started a fire to heat some broth for Morris, something to make him drowsy so that he wouldn't hurt himself worse trying to help against the rustlers.

"You do what you can to stop Watt," Molly said. "I can take care of Ben. Whiskey and I will be fine."

Lassiter knew it would take all the hands to get the main herd back under control and drive off Watt and his men. They would just have to sacrifice the longhorns that were bogged in the soft river crossing.

Lassiter climbed on his stallion. He was still worried about Molly and Morris and Whiskey, but he knew the herd would be lost if he didn't lead the hands after Watt and the others right away.

With a gun in his right hand, Lassiter rode to the front of the herd. Here and there a running battle between a rustler and one of the hands would take place. The hands were so angered that they took chances, and usually got the best of the fight.

Lassiter surged ahead on his black. Just ahead of him were two of the rustlers, who turned on him as he rode up. Their eyes were huge and they shot wildly as Lassiter extended his arm.

The first blast took the rustler nearest him squarely in the head as he was turned to fire. The rustlers head snapped sideways and he flipped from the horse and under the stampeding herd.

The second rustler was riding between Lassiter and the herd, with no place to go. Instead of coming out and facing Lassiter, the rustler tried to work his horse into the crazed, surging longhorns.

The horse stumbled immediately. The rustler plunged head-first into the ranging horns and hooves, while the horse kept its footing and ran with the herd.

Lassiter moved ahead again, this time shooting in front of the lead steers to try and turn them into each other and slow them down. He succeeded in getting them to turn slightly, heading for a tributary stream that lay just a half mile ahead.

The stream would tend to slow the herd considerably, Lassiter knew, if he could get the lead animals to turn just a little more.

Two more Bar 9 hands rode up to help him. They yelled to him that most of the rustlers had been killed or wounded, but that no one had been able to get Watt. He was somewhere behind them, back where they had tried to ford the cattle through the quicksand—where Molly and Whiskey were attending Morris.

Lassiter told the hands that they could stop the herd if they continued to turn them in a circle and get them to see the tributary stream ahead of them. It was wide enough that they could plunge in and not be hurt. The only worry would be quicksand again.

Lassiter turned his horse and started back toward the wagon. He was out from the herd, pushing his black into full speed. Ahead of him a running battle between two Bar 9 hands and four of the rustlers was taking place.

The four rustlers would be enough to get the herd back into a full stampede if they managed to get to the front of the herd. Lassiter knew he would have to stop them from killing the hands and getting to the front. They were already bearing down on the hands and Lassiter knew if they succeeded in killing them, the herd might be lost.

When the four rustlers saw Lassiter coming toward them, they fanned out in two directions to try and come at him from both sides. Two of them swung out from the river, while the other two made their move from alongside the herd.

The two hands joined Lassiter and turned to face the two that were coming from the river. Lassiter took the two that came at him from the herd.

They were trained fighters, and they tried to shoot at Lassiter from both sides as they rode toward him. But Lassiter leaned down across the side of his horse and, at the last instant, swung the black stallion into the path of one oncoming rustler.

The rustler's horse balked and Lassiter rose up and shot him from the saddle. The other rustler was going past and before he could get a good shot off, Lassiter had turned the stallion and was chasing him.

The rustler knew he had no chance now and spurred his horse as hard as he could. He was headed right for the river and Lassiter could see he did not intend to stop his horse.

At the edge of the river, the horse stopped, throwing the rustler into the water. The rustler tried to get up, but found himself caught helplessly in quicksand. He yelled and stretched his arms out for help as the water poured over him and took him under.

Lassiter turned from the river and headed once more toward the chuck wagon. As he rode ahead, Lassiter could see Watt and two of his men coming toward the wagons from the dust that surrounded the herd. Lassiter considered that Watt most likely thought the herd was now under control and he could take his time going for the wagon.

It occurred to Lassiter that Watt had no doubt seen Molly by now and was going to do with her what he wanted. Lassiter did not think coming straight at Watt would do any good; besides, the odds were against him, especially when one of the three was someone who could shoot like Watt.

Instead, Lassiter reined his stallion in under the cover of the trees along the river and headed through the cover for the wagon. He would see if he couldn't get there in time to help Molly and Whiskey. But he would have to hurry.

20

MOLLY WAS JUST GETTING the broth down Morris and watching him relax when she heard Whiskey yelling from just outside the wagon.

"Rustlers!" he told her. "Stay in the wagon and keep your head down!"

Whiskey took cover underneath the wagon and Molly rummaged in her big bag for the Colt Dragoon. She could hear shooting outside, and she lowered herself over Morris as two bullets zipped through the canvas of the wagon.

Deeply angered, Molly cocked the hammer back on the Colt and raised herself up to look out the back. Two rustlers were circling the wagon, trying to get a clear shot at Whiskey underneath. He was cursing at them, firing his rifle. But they were moving targets and he couldn't safely expose himself to get a clear shot at them.

Molly waited until the two rustlers circled the wagon again. Then she stood up in the back of the wagon and leaned out, aiming the colt and holding it with both hands. The one in the lead noticed her and held his horse up, his face showing surprise. Molly brought the big Colt up and fired.

The rustler clutched at his front and began to gasp. He brought his own weapon up, but fired wildly past Molly through the back of the wagon. She cocked the Colt again.

The second rustler had stopped to get a shot off at Molly and was now tumbling off his horse, as Whiskey's Winchester boomed from under the wagon. Molly shot the first rustler again, this time hitting him in the neck. He jerked a few times and Molly shot again, the bullet taking him through the heart. He was dead before he hit the ground.

She watched for more rustlers as Morris started talking from where he was lying down. He was too drowsy to fight, but wanted her to help him come awake.

"We've got it under control," she told Morris.

"Molly, don't get hurt," he said to her.

She went over to where he was looking up at her. He continued to stare at her, his eyes telling her that he cared a great deal, but had never wanted to express it.

"Let me help you," he said.

But she kept him down, insisting that he stay put and not aggravate the wound anymore—not if he ever wanted to walk again.

There was one more rustler who showed himself now, and Molly could hear Whiskey yelling at him to stay back. It was Morgan Watt.

"What's the matter, old man, you afraid?" Watt taunted.

Watt was getting down from his horse. He had a rifle and he seemed totally confident.

Watt began walking toward the wagon. He knew

Whiskey was going to shoot at him. But the angle was bad and when Whiskey had to expose himself for the shot, then he would kill him. It was the woman he wanted.

He hadn't known there was a woman along. She must have joined them at Dallas. But that was to his favor; if he could get to her, he would have a good chance at getting Lassiter.

Whiskey watched Watt advance and knew if he got into position for a decent shot, Watt would have a better shot. And Watt rarely missed.

Instead of taking a chance, Whiskey came out the other side of the wagon and yelled for Molly to get down, that Watt wouldn't stop for anything.

"I'll shoot him when he gets close enough," Molly said. "He's crazy to just be walking toward us like that."

"I'll shoot him," came a voice from behind her.

Molly turned to see Lassiter climb up into the wagon from the other side. She was startled, but happy at the same time.

"Some of the hands told me Watt was back here," Lassiter said. "I decided to surprise him."

Lassiter checked to see how Morris was doing. He was glad to see Morris was feeling well enough to talk.

"Just go to your knitting," Lassiter suggested to Morris. "This will all be over soon."

Watt was still strolling toward the wagon. But he had slowed some, wondering what he was going to have to face now. He couldn't see inside the wagon, and he knew the woman hadn't gotten out to run. Maybe she was cowering somewhere inside with Morris. He smiled.

Then Watt stopped in his tracks when he saw Lassiter suddenly jump down from the back. He was so startled that he nearly dropped the rifle. Then he decided to drop it anyway, as it would do him little good now.

Lassiter walked a few steps forward and stopped. He was waiting, his hands hovering near his twin Colt revolvers.

"You told me once I was pretty slow," Lassiter told Watt. "Now maybe you want to show me how fast you are."

Watt had recovered some from his surprise. He began to think about the incident in the saloon when Johnson had pulled on Lassiter. Johnson's gun hadn't cleared the holster when he was dead from Lassiter's bullets. Now Watt was sure that Lassiter had pulled slow, just to fool him.

But then he began to think—as he had at the time—that Lassiter had drawn as fast as he knew how. He had to think that way, for he was going to have to kill Lassiter now, or die trying.

"I'm waiting," Lassiter said. "Or do you just want to hang?"

"You'll never live to see me hang," Watt told him. "In fact, this is your last moment of life."

Watt went for his gun with incredible speed. But Lassiter had anticipated the moment and had his right hand filled with the weight of the black-handled Colt before Watt could bring the barrel of his own weapon out of the holster.

Watt was as fast as he had boasted and was bringing his pistol into line to fire when Lassiter's Colt filled the air with smoke. Watt felt the slug hammer his chest cavity, causing his finger to grip the trigger of his own pistol, discharging it into the dirt at his feet.

With blurry eyes, Watt then saw Lassiter bring his left hand over and begin fanning the hammer of his revolver. It was as if it was happening in slow motion—

the successive blasts from the Colt, the repeated stabs of pain as the bullets riddled his heart and lungs.

Then all was black as Morgan Watt slumped forward onto his stomach.

Whiskey came around the wagon, his eyes showing disbelief. He stared at Lassiter.

"I ain't never saw a man shoot a gun like that. Never."

Lassiter noted in Whiskey's eyes a kind of strange question, as if asking himself whether this man called Lassiter was really human, or just a machine that fired a gun far better than any human ever could.

He saw it in Molly's eyes, too. The question, the disbelief, the distance growing between them. It happened every time somebody saw him draw. They just couldn't think that he was actually one of them after that.

Lassiter reloaded his gun and slipped it back into its holster. Molly went back into the wagon to see how Morris was doing, and Whiskey met one of the hands coming from the herd.

"We've got them contained," Lassiter heard the hand telling Whiskey. "And we're going to take them across the river."

Lassiter rode out and helped bring the herd back to the main crossing. The ford was easy and after getting the steers that hadn't drowned out of the other crossing, the herd was safely grazing on the north shore.

As evening approached, the hands all gathered to talk about the day. Those who had sustained wounds had Molly treat them. Morris was sitting up again, eating from a tin plate. His hip pained him, but he was far luckier than he had reason to hope for.

But Lassiter could sense that things had become the way they always did when he had used his guns. Everyone was a little distanced from him now, wondering if he could ever get that mad at them. They had heard about his lightning draw against Watt. Though it was the most relaxed night of the drive, Lassiter felt somehow out of place.

Lassiter thought about his place among them and concluded it would be best if he rode on right away, now that there was nothing to worry about the rest of the way to Dodge City.

He had made some good friends and he wanted them to remember him as just one of them. He didn't like to think they would segregate him, though that's what always happened.

Lassiter found Whiskey and told him that he would miss his beef and beans. The old cook laughed.

"I wish you good luck," he told Lassiter.

Lassiter then found Molly washing supper dishes.

"You won't have any trouble finding your mother in Dodge City," Lassiter told her. "Have a nice stay with her."

Molly wanted to come toward Lassiter, but restrained herself.

"I won't forget you," she said.

"I hope you can stay happy," Lassiter told her.

"Will I ever see you again?" Molly asked.

"I hope so," Lassiter answered. "Someday, someplace. I hope so."

Morris had known Lassiter likely wouldn't stay until the end of the drive. That's the way Lassiter was, and there was nothing wrong with that. The man just didn't feel comfortable in one place too long.

"What about your pay?" Morris asked while Lassiter got his black stallion ready to ride.

"Give it to Molly to help with her mother," Lassiter said. "I'd just spend it all."

Morris laughed. "You've always held tight rein on your money. I'm the one you should worry about."

"Stay away from the poker tables," Lassiter advised.

"You don't have to worry about me gambling mine away this time," Morris told Lassiter with a laugh. "I can't sit on this hip for longer than a few minutes at a time. Guess I'll just be content to lay around camp."

"That will be the first time you've ever done that," Lassiter said. "Save your money and start your own spread."

Morris nodded. "I aim to. Will you help me run it?"

Lassiter climbed into the saddle. "I'll check in on you from time to time."

Morris nodded. "See you up the trail somewhere."

Lassiter rode his black stallion from camp and out onto the trail that led up to Dodge City. He would likely stay at Camp Supply for the night, and go on until he passed the cowtowns and then farther north. Where he would end up, he had no idea. But he wouldn't forget where he had been and the friends he had made with the Bar 9 outfit.

THE BEST WESTERN NOVELS COME FROM POCKET BOOKS

Loren Zane Grey

☐ AMBUSH FOR LASSITER .... 52885/$2.95
☐ A GRAVE FOR LASSITER .... 62724/$2.95
☐ LASSITER .... 52886/$2.95
☐ LASSITER ON THE TEXAS TRAIL ...... 63894/$2.95
☐ LASSITER GOLD .... 60780/$2.95
☐ LASSITER TOUGH .... 60781/$2.95
☐ THE LASSITER LUCK .... 62723/$2.95
☐ LASSITER'S RIDE .... 63892/$2.95

Loren D. Estleman

☐ THE HIDER .... 64905/$2.75
☐ HIGH ROCKS .... 63846/$2.75
☐ MURDOCK'S LAW .... 44951/$2.75
☐ THE STAMPING GROUND .... 64479/$2.75
☐ THE WOLFER .... 66144/$2.75

Norman A. Fox

☐ THIRSTY LAND .... 64816/$2.75
☐ SHADOW ON THE RANGE .... 64817/$2.75

Frank O'Rourke

☐ AMBUSCADE .... 63684/$2.75
☐ BLACKWATER .... 63687/$2.75
☐ HIGH VENGEANCE .... 63686/$2.75
☐ LATIGO .... 63682/$2.75
☐ THE PROFESSIONALS .... 63683/$2.75
☐ VIOLENCE AT SUNDOWN .... 63685/$2.75

William Dedecker

☐ TO BE A MAN .... 64936/$2.75
☐ THE HOLDOUTS .... 64937/$2.75

Owen Wister

☐ THE VIRGINIAN .... 46757/$3.95

POCKET BOOKS

Simon & Schuster Mail Order Dept. WPB
200 Old Tappan Rd., Old Tappan, N.J. 07675

Please send me the books I have checked above. I am enclosing $_____ (please add 75¢ to cover postage and handling for each order. N.Y.S. and N.Y.C. residents please add appropriate sales tax). Send check or money order--no cash or C.O.D.'s please. Allow up to six weeks for delivery. For purchases over $10.00 you may use VISA: card number, expiration date and customer signature must be included.

Name _____

Address _____

City _____ State/Zip _____

VISA Card No. _____ Exp. Date _____

Signature _____ 290-02

FROM POCKET BOOKS AND BOOK CREATIONS, INC. COMES AN EXCITING NEW WESTERN SERIES

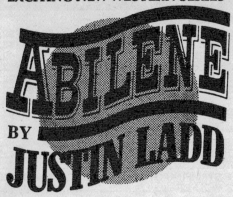

ABILENE
BY JUSTIN LADD

In the powerful tradition of TV's "Gunsmoke" comes *ABILENE*, a compelling mix of great storytelling and action adventure in a continuing series.

Don't miss out on the action with a new *ABILENE* adventure every other month!

☐ **BOOK I: THE PEACEMAKER**
64897/$2.95

☐ **BOOK II: THE SHARPSHOOTER**
64898/$2.95

☐ **BOOK III: THE PURSUERS**
64899/$2.95

☐ **BOOK IV: THE NIGHT RIDERS**
64900/$2.95

Simon & Schuster Mail Order Dept. AJL
200 Old Tappan Rd., Old Tappan, N.J. 07675

POCKET
BOOKS

Please send me the books I have checked above. I am enclosing $_____ (please add 75¢ to cover postage and handling for each order. N.Y.S. and N.Y.C. residents please add appropriate sales tax). Send check or money order--no cash or C.O.D.'s please. Allow up to six weeks for delivery. For purchases over $10.00 you may use VISA: card number, expiration date and customer signature must be included.

Name _____

Address _____

City _____ State/Zip _____

VISA Card No. _____ Exp. Date _____

Signature _____ 292-03